I0659148

THE KEEP
2020

VISIONS OF NEW CASTLE

THE KEEP: VISIONS OF NEW CASTLE

2020 EDITORS

SUSAN URBANEK LINVILLE

BRITTANY LINVILLE TONET

COVER PHOTOS BY SUSAN URBANEK LINVILLE

COVER DESIGN BY STEPHEN V. RAMEY

INTERIOR DESIGN BY STEPHEN V. RAMEY

FIRST PRINTING DECEMBER 2020

ISBN: 978-1-951847-02-9

PRINTED IN THE UNITED STATES OF AMERICA

Contents

Contributors

working to a deadline, you see, and she hasn't turned up. We were supposed to meet over there." He turned and pointed to a seat in the square. "That was over an hour ago. She's let me down." He paused again. "Again, I'm *so* sorry. I must be coming across as some sort of creep. I'll let you go. Bye, bye." He smiled, turned and walked halfway back to the seat while watching her reflection in the far side shop mirror. He stopped, made a display of checking his watch and tapped his foot impatiently. He glanced around then briefly smiled at her again awkwardly, before moving further away and stopping. Then he took out his phone and made as if he was checking for messages.

Helen turned and entered the shop. He waited patiently, keeping his eyes on the reflections rather than looking directly at her. He figured she might be checking him out.

After about ten minutes she re-appeared, this time holding a small bag, so she must have purchased something. Obviously, it was something she didn't want the clown to know about. A present maybe? He rose and turned and their eyes met. Then just before she could walk away, he held his hand up and ran over to her.

"I'm sorry to impose... and I know it's a cheek, but I wonder if you have... do you have a moment?"

Again, she looked at him blankly.

"Am I holding you up?"

She slowly shook her head.

"Wonderful. Look, my name is Evan. Evan Stephenson, here's my card..." He reached into his coat pocket and as he pulled out a business card, a

Introduction

Welcome to the second annual edition of *The Keep: Visions of New Castle*. Covid has certainly left its mark on our production schedule, but we did manage to get it out before Christmas season, which was always our goal. Thanks to the contributors who continue to make this collection possible, and thanks to you, dear reader, who make the undertaking worthwhile.

New Castle is a western Pennsylvania city that sits in the middle of the rust belt. Like many towns in the region, loss of manufacturing jobs led to economic decline. It is time for that decline end. Following in the footsteps of Pittsburgh and Youngstown, the city must now rise from the ashes. Pokeberry Press is here to be one of the many forces that will bring it back to life.

When we were thinking about a title for our New Castle anthology, we wanted something to reflect New Castle's strength and endurance. We settled on *The Keep*.

A medieval castle keep served multiple purposes. The top of the tower was the residence of the castle's lord. The middle floor held the great hall. During late medieval times, the lower storage areas became places to incarcerate political prisoners. Finally, during invasions, the castle keep served as a defensive position since it was located at a high point that could be manned by archers.

New Castle's Keep was created to be a venue for outstanding poetry, prose, fiction, non-fiction, art and photography by novices and professionals. The only constraint is that the subject matter includes New Castle, PA in some way, be it past, present, or future.

We hope you enjoy the result.

Posts

Joseph Kearney

When I am here
I think of the ages past
The long years that come and go
And the wooden fence posts enduring
The rain and time drawing them out
Slowly to become themselves
They stand weathering year by year
Offering their silent witness to the wind
Their encased hearts to the wandering
And restless sky

Kristine DeFelice

Great Blue Heron from Moraine State Park

Late August on Croton Avenue

Sam Giannetti

"Sammy," my mother shouted with that particular sternness that often surrounded her words when she wanted me to do something, "go out and play with the other kids!"

I was leisurely watching television, resting my head on a hand supported by my elbow. It was a Saturday, late morning heading toward noon. As an adopted only child living with an older couple who took me in to fill an empty hole in the woman's life, an open wound left by her infant daughter's death two decades prior, much of my time outside of school was spent alone. I found a space on the front room rug, about three feet before the Philco floor model TV, a place where my multiple distractions could be effectively indulged. Comic books, drawing pad, a castle made out of 1955 Bowman TV baseball cards, and little soldier figurines cluttered about. It was the 1960s and I was aging into my mid-teen years.

"Get up and go out and play!" she insisted with that authority mothers believe is theirs by right. "Johnny is getting together a basketball game and they need players. You should be more social. Quit acting like a weirdo. Go out and play!"

Mom was concerned by my penchant for solitude and often urged me into neighborhood group activities. So, dutifully, I said ok because there really wasn't anything special I was watching on the tube anyway, and all this other stuff could resume at a later time. I slowly pulled myself off of the carpet. Funny, as I sit here thinking back, two different floral patterns, one upon a light and another on a dark background, come to mind. I'm sure this was a scene that repeated itself many times over the course of my adolescence, so epochal changes in the parlor rug blur in my memory.

On this specific occasion, I recall sprinting through the kitchen, then hopping down the three steps that led to the rear door. I burst out into the backyard of our little stretch of home. From where I stood, the world was bordered by the Croton Methodist Church on the north, the woods hemming the entire circumference of family properties. Casa Falcone lay to the south. George Falcone, Sr., owned most of the wooded area directly behind our houses. His eldest son George Jr., nicknamed Tippy, had joined the U.S. Navy and was off somewhere on maneuvers. Michael, the second oldest son, was the block's current alpha male.

I leapt over the cement block wall Dad had built between ours and the Scratchiano property line. Sometimes I missed rolling down the little hill that had been cut off to definitively demarcate territorial parameters for the Scratchiano and Giannetti families. The Scratchiano domain was a sort of no man's land resting between my mom, Mary, and her sister Annie's homes. The aroma that floated about that residence was so rancid that on a hot summer day it drifted all around the neighborhood.

I played with Ralph Jr. and Gabe Scratchiano occasionally but no one else in the neighborhood deemed to do so. This is why I was probably allowed to pass through their yard when travelling over to the Presuttos' to play basketball without the adults in the Scratchiano clan yelling at me. Davey Buck, my other next-door neighbor, walked down the front sidewalk to join in the game. He had two older brothers who, like Tippy, no longer lived at home. Only Davey and Danny Buck still lived there. Danny would only play football with the group because he didn't like basketball. Davey, however, would try his hand at this game from time to time.

Michael Falcone was a central figure in this blacktop driveway league. He could be described as testosterone on two legs. The muscles of his sinewy forearms were something to behold, exhibiting tendons like cables built up by the repetitive painting motion made when working with his father, who operated a small paint and wallpaper store. He was a wavy-haired charismatic Pan-like character. Girls from across the street would often stroll over to the Presuttos' yard to steal glances at the blond Italian Adonis of our block during these games.

Johnny and Richard were my mom's nephews and my cousins-in-law as an adopted foundling. Johnny was the older brother and frequent instigator who generally organized the athletic games that took place in the neighborhood. If we weren't playing softball in the dried out flat meadow hollow up over the wooded hill or football on either the Presutto or Falcone lawns, then it was basketball on the blacktop driveway in front of Johnny's family garage. His father, Uncle Mario, was a really gracious man who, like my dad, spoke broken English. He really was fairly indulgent regarding our games. His only prohibition for us was not messing up his beautiful garden adjacent to both the lawn and driveway where our games ensued. More often than he liked, a stray pass would end up in the middle of his tomatoes or onions. Even the most surgical fetching of a ball was considered akin to the sin of Adam by Uncle Mario.

Lastly, Ronnie Exposito from up the street came down to play at Johnny's court. This was quite a feather for my cousin, giving him incredible neighborhood street cred because Ronnie was the sixth man on the high school basketball team, renowned for his long shot. Richard and I, among the youngest along with several others like Nunzio Biondi, rounded out the roster for these Saturday afternoon competitions. Michael and Johnny were the captains who picked teams. On this occasion, Richard and I were on Johnny's side along with Davey Buck. Mike, who had won the first pick, took Ronnie.

The Presuttos shared a garage and driveway with the Scratchianos upon which hung a makeshift backboard and hoop. Ralph Sr. wasn't disposed to support the basketball games that infringed on his part of the property. He demonstrated his displeasure by parking his beat-up car directly in front of the garage door. This vehicle was formerly a yellow Taxi cab painted and modified to look like a regular vehicle. He just showed up with it one day. Ralphie told me he'd gotten it from New York. To make matters worse, Ralph Sr.'s wife's father, Carmanooche, sat nearby beneath the grape arbor smoking a cigar and glaring at us as we played.

Carmanooche was slight in build but fearful in demeanor when he came home inebriated from the Sons of Italy club on Friday nights staggering out of a cab dressed in his suit. He'd hunch over, screaming curses in his native tongue at anyone in sight while brandishing the four-inch blade he always carried in his pocket. There were some whispered tales that he came to America after a fight back in Sicily resulting in the death of some local foe. No one knew for sure. The irreverent Ronnie, who was shielded from the repercussions of his flippant tongue because he lived up on Cascade Street, pronounced the old man's name Almondcrunch which had become a running joke with the gang. To say that Carmanooche disliked most of the kids in the neighborhood is probably an understatement.

Often when I was doing my chore of burning garbage behind our garage near to the woods, Carmanooche would be sitting on a little stool by a compost heap he'd nurtured smoking a Parodi cigar. I'd stroll over and say hello sometimes or at least acknowledge his presence. When, on occasion, I'd get close enough to feign a conversation, my inability to understand his Italian-American mishmash made any actual understanding impossible. But he seemed to appreciate the respect and interest that I showed for him at these times.

So, on this particular Saturday, Ralph the elder moved his car in front of the garage just as we began the basketball game, taking away Ronnie's favorite corner spot for shooting. The engagement was fairly heated. Michael sarcastically thanked Ralph Sr. for this detrimental act. Mr. Scratchiano ignored the comment as he closed the car door and walked toward his house. Uncle Mario was out for the afternoon shopping with Aunt Annie so there was no adult influence to stave off the events of that day.

Whenever Richard or I missed a shot and the turnover resulted in Michael's team scoring points, Johnny acted out the ritual of bouncing whichever of us who was the offender off the garage door. This occurred soon after the tip off when Richard took an outside shot that bounced off the rusting orange rim. Mike got the rebound and passed the ball to Ronnie at half court because the court rule was that you couldn't take a shot recovered from an opponent's possession without first bringing it back behind the imaginary line projected from the little cement block wall that hemmed Uncle Mario's garden. Ronnie gracefully took the shot and it swished right through the hoop with the weather-beaten net waving in acknowledgment.

"You stupid little idiot!" Johnny shouted as he pushed Richard into the wooden garage door.

Like the wrestlers we watched on Channel 11, Richard and I feigned more damage from this punishment than actually occurred, so as to reduce the vehemence of the next sanction. I tossed the ball back into play to our captain, a strategy Johnny employed to reduce my hands on it during the action. He dribbled about three steps and let go a shot. It banked off the backboard and passed through the hoop. The game was quickly tied up.

The tide continued to swing back and forth. When the game was tied at 12 all, Ronnie missed a shot that careened off the side of the hoop, sailed through the Scratchiano grape arbor and landed in the middle of Carmanooche's tomato patch in the adjacent garden. He was sitting at a picnic table set beneath the grape arbor peeling an apple with his pocket knife. The game stopped and all of us huddled around in a group furtively glancing at the brown ball inertly sitting conspicuously out of place.

Michael was the first to address the problem calling out to the old man. "Can we get our ball?"

Carmanooche continued shaving the skin from his apple while ignoring Mike's question. A few seconds of silence went by.

"What'll we do?" Mike asked turning back to the circle of players.

Johnny took the initiative and walked over toward the grape arbor. "Mr. Chicco," he started, "can we please get our ball?"

The old man raised his head and looked over at his neighbor. We all heard sounds emanating from Carmanooche's mouth, but the garbled mixture of English and Italian was unrecognizable except for one word, "Sammy."

Johnny turned toward me and said "I think he'll let you get the ball for us."

It seemed like all eyes were turned toward me. At that moment, I wished that I were still on the floor in front of the television set. I slowly walked over to the picnic table. Carmanooche got up and gingerly went into the garden, picked up the ball and brought it out to me.

I carried the ball back to the court where I was greeted with "way to goes" and other compliments. Being nice to the old man paid off, I guess.

I don't know if it was because my self-esteem was increased as a result of the heroic glow or if the hours of lone shooting in the hoop in my parents' yard really improved my accuracy, but the next three times Johnny passed the ball to me my shots fell through the hoop. Six points in a row. Richard didn't have that kind of luck. His shots either bounced off the rim or sailed over the backboard resulting in a severe door bouncing after the third miss. Johnny sank the final shot winning the game and our team broke out into wild celebration. In a very uncharacteristic act, Johnny slapped me on the back and told me what a great job I did.

All of a sudden, Richard came over and took a violent swing at me. I stepped back and his fist cut through the air. I saw red. Here was my younger cousin, who I had known all his life, trying to use me like a punching bag.

We weren't very close anymore. Often, we'd played cowboys and Indians or army in our early grade school days. As we became older, we began drifting off toward other groups of kids. Richard was embraced by the neighborhood crew. Michael had bequeathed his job working at Jamison's Ice Cream & Candy Store up the block to Richard. My old classmates, Tracy Gardner and Gary Garrett, had transferred their loyalties to Richard. I was more of an odd duck with interests quite different from the homeboys. The new friends I inclined toward were more likely to live on the North Hill or be musician wannabees.

His fit of anger could have been triggered by being shown up in front of his peer group. My response was perhaps the realization that I was not really a member of his family.

Without thinking, I just lashed back, punching him right in the face. Richard hollered more in surprise than pain and ran crying into his house.

Nothing like this had ever happened with us before. Everyone just stood silently watching the scene.

That moment, in retrospect, was a tipping point for me. Something had changed. This was when I severed my connection with the neighborhood culture or, at least, it signaled a change. This was the end of my childhood and graduation to a world beyond Croton Avenue.

Tribute to Lawrence County CARES Center

Lavonne Lyles

I could spend my life counting my sorrows, and that's usually
what I do.

But I started counting my blessings, when I count you.

I could measure every raindrop and never see the sun,

A life of melancholy, without no fun.

But you changed my perspective, you changed everything I see.

I thank Lawrence County CARES, 'cause you changed me.

Love never fails.

My First Job

Colleen Seegers

When you are an eight-year-old girl in a small town like New Castle, PA, your job possibilities are pretty slim. You can imagine my joy when a neighbor offered me a job picking strawberries for the amazing sum of ten cents for every quart I picked. I had visions of candy, comic books, bubble gum, and extra money in my pocket.

I arrived bright and early to the small lot up the road from my house. It was well kept with mounds of clean straw between the rows of bushy green plants loaded with bright berries. I was handed three baskets to begin my way to wealth. Down on my knees, I started to pick. That straw looked pretty, but my knees didn't think it was as soft as it looked with each move I made.

I accidentally squashed part of a berry, so I popped it in my mouth to hide the evidence. It was so sweet and juicy. It opened a Pandora's box of sorts. For every five or six berries put in the basket, one went in my mouth. The "boss" (Mrs. Anderson), must have seen me because there she was, hands on hips at the edge of the field, "You're not eating those, are you?"

Wiping the juice from my chin, I meekly answered, "No".

She gave me a snarl and went back in her house. I finished filling that basket. A great idea came to me. If I lay flat while I picked, my eating would not be able to be seen. A short time later, another reprimand. With the second basket filled, Mrs. Anderson told me it was time to go home for lunch. I didn't even notice it was ten thirty.

I skipped down the road to my house. My Mother didn't seem impressed when I told her how good the berries were. She gave me a small snack.

While I was eating, she said, "Mrs. Anderson called me before you got home. She said you can't go back to pick. You ate too many berries."

I did go back for my twenty cents.

The Haunted Hill View Manor

Kat Rodgers

Shadows of the past greet guests at the threshold of 2801 Ellwood Road, New Castle, PA. The stately structure exists as one of the most haunted places in New Castle, a steadfast home to paranormal and ghostly activity. The entities are welcome here at the Hill View Manor.

One might ask how or why this happens. Many ghost hunters believe that deceased entities haunt sources of personal pain and suffering to relay their past life stories to the living. They want us to remember what happened in that location. Most often, haunting occurs in places where people have died, or bodies are buried. After nearly a century of operations at the Hill View Manor, it has been estimated that many residents died and were buried in the cemetery located on the grounds. Some graves exist unmarked, being as there were no accurate records kept on file.

The story began in 1867 with the New Castle City Home, a common working farm and home for the elderly and poor. Over time, a newer, larger facility became needed which included designs to consolidate several small county institutions. In 1925 plans for the new Lawrence County Home for the Aged were bid, accepted, designed, and built by architect A.L. Thayer.

In 1926, the new location opened on the outskirts of New Castle. It continued under the operation of the previous home's managers, Perry and Mary Snyder, who moved in with their own children, staff, and 'inmates', as they were commonly called in those days. Residents were typically permanent, homeless, mentally challenged, destitute, and elderly. Out of the ordinary, two very young brothers were taken in among the fresh clutch of dwellers due to the mergers.

The spacious three-story building was built to house 110 residents. Men lived in the West wing, women in the East wing, with a hospital, laundry, and kitchen. It included a bomb shelter, cemetery, and a small working farm.

The Snyders ran this poor house and farm from 1926-1944 before Mantz B. Hogue took charge of the operations. The Snyders were forced to leave after their incompetence and corruption was uncovered. Their recordkeeping was not updated and accurate. A severe storm swept through the cemetery, washing up many bodies that had been improperly buried, with no records on file.

In the 1960's, the enterprise gradually transitioned into a skilled nursing center. A North wing addition was built and completed around 1977 to accommodate thirty more patients due to overcrowding issues. It was at that time the Lawrence County Home for the Aged was renamed as Hill View Manor.

Financial problems brought the operations to an end in 2004 after 78 years of being 'home' to hundreds of residents. It was usually where they lived an entire life, passed, and were buried in the cemetery out back. However, the spirits of some patients have always remained, keeping its history and their memories alive.

The real estate sat idle until a woman from Pittsburgh purchased it in 2005. Her intentions were to renovate the building into apartments or a condominium. Unfortunately, the new owner passed away within the year.

Upon her death, the property was inherited by the family, who had no idea what to do with it. They soon heard the haunted stories from years gone by, when workers of the facility witnessed paranormal activity during daily operations. For several years, the family was approached by ghost hunters to explore the building. In 2013, they began doing business as Haunted Hill View Manor ghost tours. This preserved its integrity and legacy as a haunted estate. The doors re-opened as an ideal spot for skeptics, adventurers, and paranormal investigators to experience the spooky, spine-chilling elements that manifest within. It has gained popularity as the Haunted Hill View Manor, a forever home to those shadows of a past existence.

Ghost Hunter, Travel Channel's *Ghost Adventures, Ghost Lab, Destination Fear, The Spirit Realm Network,* SyFy's *Ghost Hunters,* and, most recently, *Destination Fear* are among the popular investigators that have visited. Using scientific gadgets, professionals and enthusiasts attempt to understand supernatural events.

Instruments used to hunt and interact with ghosts include thermal scanners, motion and infrared sensors, dowsing rods, infrared lights, EVP's (electronic voice phenomena), EMF meters to detect electromagnetic fields, night vision cameras, video cams, LED flashlights, pen, paper, and extra alkaline batteries. The entities are known to drain batteries for their needed energy.

While nothing has been scientifically proven about ghosts, spirits, and other strange paranormal events, it remains an ongoing challenge steeped in investigative findings, speculation, and personal opinions or beliefs. In the deep dive into the paranormal phenomenon; the best is yet to come.

According to www.astronomynotes.com, the answer boils down to scientific truth vs. religious truths, which tends to cause confusion and conflict among people. Scientific truth is based on clear observation of physical reality and can be tested. Many religious truths are held to be true no matter what: like God's existence.

Paranormal encounters are always active at the Haunted Hill View Manor. It's commonly said that "if the walls could only talk." Aren't they trying to? Could it really be the spirits of former occupants reaching out to tell their horrors of confinement within those echoing walls?

The current owner and their investigative team recounted undocumented stories of unusual personal incidents and interactions with entities which occurred as she prepared to open the building to the public. One of the owners alongside Nick, the alarm system tech and electrician, were checking out the electrical panels. A disc, vital for electricity was missing from the breaker box. Nick commented that it was a shame they couldn't get it up and running that day. They traveled through the hallways inspecting the electrical work. Both men felt a cold entity trailing behind them from time to time.

After their rounds, they reopened the box with the missing disc to get a replacement measurement. To their surprise, the disc had reappeared intact. Both men scratched their heads, felt a strong chill run down their spines, and got a strong whiff of an invisible cigar. On the way home, the owner called his sister, "You're not going to believe this..."

Since then, they discovered that the electrical box is located in Eli's hallway. They credit this spirit for having something to do with its mysterious return.

The next day, an owner hung huge directional signs throughout the building. She assembled a couple old Polaroid pictures of former residents on the wall. Later, as she brushed by them, she noticed someone had put up another photo showing two men she hadn't seen prior. She inquired. Her brother remarked that he didn't pin it. He was too busy for that. Days later, a visitor identified one of the two men as Jimmy, a former third floor resident who was there from the poor house to the nursing home. He was touted to be a prankster and loved trading Polaroids for cigarettes. The other man in the photo was said to be his cohort, Jewels. The owner enlarged the photo. It became noticed by a different family member. Jewels was not in the photo. It was Lester. The facility welcomes stories and facts about the residents from those who worked there or knew them.

The current owner suffered an unexpected death of her brother. She commented about her heartfelt loss without him in her life and at the manor. Nothing had ever frightened him. He honestly didn't believe in ghosts, spirits, or entities and sluffed off weird things as merely coincidental or explainable. She always felt added protection when he used to be there with her in the dark, creepy corridors and basement.

Not long after her brother passed, she chaperoned a psychic tour investigation with a medium guiding the group. The medium encountered a gentle male spirit that was worried about someone in the bunch with ankle problems who refused to stay off her feet and take it easy. When the medium asked if anyone knew who this could be, silence followed. She spoke up and asked if it was her brother. The medium nodded, "He wants you to know that he now believes."

From the beginning of this entrepreneurship, the entities have established beneficial relationships with a new owner, staff, volunteers, tour guides, and in-house paranormal investigators.

The Haunted Hill View Manor parcel has gained status on the list of popular places with the greatest paranormal activity.

Plans for future growth include but are not limited to:
- In house psychic medium communication availability for scheduled readings.
- Try before you buy. Learn/use the various equipment of the professionals in real ghost hunting investigations.
- Sponsorship of brand name clothing/equipment.
- Chartered bus trips to explore/network with other haunted local places.
- On site charity functions.
- Availability as motorcycle poker run stops.
- Guest speakers and tours.
- Mini-classes and mini-tours.
- Frequent psychic fairs.
- Fright night! Share captured film footage/ghost stories over popcorn.
- Expanded gift shop selection.
- Continued options for outside/inside; private/public investigations and tour lengths.
- Continued lock-ins and private parties/functions including weddings, graduation parties...

- Halloween Scare House & other special holiday events.
- National Ghost Hunting Day.
- Paranormal Book Fairs.
- Sunday Rummage Sales.
- Annual Hill-Con Day.
- World's Largest Ghost Hunt.
- Public Psychic Investigations.
- Public Investigations with The Spirit Realm Network.
- Howling Night Tours.

Open to the public for business, this stately manor rightfully stretches across the hilltop situated on thirteen acres along Route 65 South. Its 80,000 plus square foot dwelling will always be considered "home to those who once lived there and continue to reside, even after death."
Photos courtesy of Hillview Manor

Halloween Memory

MaryAnne Gavrile

Every Halloween, my mother would make our costumes and I would cry because I wanted to be like everyone else: go to Gaylord's and buy one in a box. One year, when I was three and my brother was five, she made us Uncle Sam and Mrs. Uncle Sam costumes out of crepe paper that she sewed.

She entered us in the costume contest at the Manos theater. I cried the whole time, from walking to the theater to being on stage.

We won first place!! This emboldened her to continually make our costumes: clowns, pumpkins, zombies, etc. I still wanted a costume from a box, but I realized now how special this was. Her message was, never be like everyone else…be creative and one of a kind.

In memory of my mother, Antonetta Butchelle Gavrile.

Living Coal and Steel

Susan Urbanek Linville

They sailed in steerage
Those huddled masses
Yearning to be free
Wops, Polaks, Honkies
Dreaming golden streets
Living coal and steel
Their calloused hands
Coaxed iron furnaces
Into erupting smelters
Their blood and bone
Filled rocky tombs
Collapsed without warning
Sweat tempered I-beams
Birthed riveted towers
Forged tracks and trestles
Stretched from sea to sea
They sailed in steerage
Those men with soot-blackened faces
Lifting this country up
Until their backs gave way

Harry the Hermit

Betty Hoover DiRisio

Harry Stein was born on May 12, 1903 to Isaac and Harriet Stein in Wampum. He made his home in the Turkey Hill section of Shenango Township, a very remote area, near the old Tindall Cemetery.

Apparently single all his life, he was a devout Christian. He taught Sunday school to young boys at West Pittsburg Methodist and had a 40-year perfect attendance record, himself. Nearly blind, he couldn't drive, and walked to church every Sunday.

In the mid-1960s, he retired from Wampum Tile and started spinning scary yarns which he loved telling local young folks. It is believed that he used the names found on headstones in the nearby cemetery to create his tales. The best-known folklore he is credited with creating is that of the fictional witch, Mary Black. He compiled his tales into a manuscript, "Memoirs of a Backcountry School."

Teenagers in the 1960s and 1970s would venture out on the darkest nights to visit "Harry the Hermit" as he became known. We would bring offerings of cakes and cookies to show our goodwill and he would invite us into his living room where he would tell his tales. His folklore made him a legend in the area.

Unfortunately, not all visitors came with good intent. In August 1968, two 25-year-old men entered his home after convincing him that he knew them. Once inside, the men beat him and forced him to give them his wallet. A month later two men again broke down his door. The men fled when Harry fired a 12-gauge shotgun at them.

In March 1969, while walking home in the evening from West Pittsburg, he was offered a ride. Two men robbed him of his change purse and stole his eye glasses. They dropped him off somewhere in Shenango township. When he returned home, he discovered his house had been entered through a cellar door. His 12-gauge shotgun and his money were missing. In November of that year, he was again robbed at his home by two men and a girl who tied him up.

He said the voice sounded like that of a man who had robbed him before. They had come to the home saying they were two couples who wanted to visit him. After they tied him with his belt, the other beat him about the face, requiring a trip to the hospital. In April 1970, six men from Ohio were arrested for disorderly conduct when they began yelling and calling him names.

In 1973, Harry had undergone surgery and was recuperating at Golden Hill Nursing home. While there, a fire destroyed his house. Cause of fire: unknown. He ended up at Hillview Manor where he died on September 5, 1980 at the age of 77. He is buried at Savanah Cemetery.

Photos courtesy of Betty Hoover DiRisio

Cascade Connections

Debra R. Sanchez

Recently I saw that the old Cascade Park swimming pool may be renovated and reopened. That news reminded me of "school picnics" at Cascade when I went to Laurel. I remembered the stories that my grandmother used to tell me about how she and her friends would take a "streetcar" from Lawrenceville in Pittsburgh, where her family ran "The Bath House" (now a historic landmark) to Lawrence County to spend the day at Cascade. It was her favorite amusement park back in the 1920s.

It also brought back memories of swimming lessons back in the early 1970s. They were taught by the Red Cross and came a little late. Other memories resurfaced, memories that I cannot escape.

I now live a couple of blocks from a lock on the Allegheny; a hungry river that took a life shortly after we moved here; a river that feeds regularly on unfortunate souls. I am constantly reminded that the river wants what the river wants. I can hear it when I step outside of my house. I watch it churn as I wait for the traffic light to turn at the end of my street.

It was early summer after 7th or 8th grade. Time has blurred the year. The youth of Eastbrook Presbyterian helped with our church's VBS (Vacation Bible School) program. My "job" was to play with the little ones during their outside recreation time. I remember how much fun we had. I remember the moment the fun ended.

Some of us were having races down the hill beside the cemetery, with the youngest kids on our backs. I tripped. The little girl on my back flew off over my head and landed hard, face down, several feet ahead of me. The adults all ran to help her. Her tears were from fear and, thankfully, she was not harmed. My tears were from fear that I had hurt her. I was relieved to be able to wipe them away.

Then I tried to stand up and they rushed back unbidden. I couldn't stand. My knee would not allow it. The adults helped me and found a place for me to rest until my mother was called to come take me to the ER. Nothing was broken, but it was a serious sprain that put me on crutches with strict orders to stay off it for a period of time.

The enforced rest was easy for me since my favorite thing to do was to sit and read. My recovery was almost complete in time for the youth group weekend retreat at a cabin somewhere along the northern part of the Allegheny. Although I was still to keep the knee wrapped, I was allowed limited walking without the crutches. It was a wonderful weekend, and each of us could bring along a friend. I invited my best friend Sherry. Her parents almost didn't let her go, but at the last minute relented.

I missed out on some of the activities, like hiking, but was able to do others, like wading in the river and floating on the innertubes. The Allegheny was fairly shallow where we were, just over waist-deep, so we were safe. We would sit in the tubes, float downstream a bit, then get off, bring them back and do it all over again. It was fun.

Until I got off at just the wrong moment.

We did not know that there was one place where the riverbed had been deepened considerably to allow for a boat launch. It was probably only as wide as a one or two-lane road. That is precisely where I got off and went under.

My knee was still weak. I did not know how to swim. The water was murky. I couldn't figure out what to do. Everything was dark, except for a circle of light. The light kept moving, closer, farther, closer, then it was gone.

I was drowning.

My mind raced. Panic set in. Then, I felt someone grab my arm and pull me onto an innertube. I woke up on the shore.

It turned out that it was Sherry who pulled me up from several feet under and held me on the innertube until one of the adults swam out and pulled me in. I owe her my life. Who knows how that would have ended if her parents hadn't changed their minds?

A few weeks later, when my knee was stronger, my parents signed my brother and me up for the Red Cross swimming lessons at Cascade Park pool. I wouldn't say that I'm a great swimmer, and you won't find me doing laps. No, I learned enough to pass the test. I can tread water and float for a very long time…in a pool.

I hope they do reopen the Cascade Park pool. There are many others who need to learn to swim. I made sure that my son and both daughters learned at an early age. They all swim better than I can.

My youngest went swimming in the Allegheny with a group of friends in the early 2010s. It was supposed to be a safe place, off the island near the Hulton Bridge where many people have cabins. It is only accessible by boat. I was worried until she was safely home. She is an excellent swimmer. But, still, I worried.

I do not like to swim in the ocean or a river. I may wade into the ocean, but not over waist deep. Knee or ankle deep is fine with me. I will not swim in a river.

I don't trust wild water. I respect it.

It is alive. It is hungry.

Easter Poem

Lavonne Lyles

Even if there was no heaven, I'd choose to go this way.

Even if there was no heaven, I'd live it day by day.

Success and riches, worldly gain, they don't appeal to me.

Somehow my mind just can't erase Him hanging on a tree.

I can't forget the sweet embrace He gave to me that day.

My heart was broken deep within from sins along the way.

In a world so all alone, He gave me peace I'd never known.

I had a joy the world can't bring; I sang a song the world can't sing.

Christ is what they're longing for – the rich and the famous, proud and poor.

The greatest that this world can offer, left me a poor, unworthy pauper.

Cherisa Rhae

Panic

Original artwork.

The Glow

Stephen V. Ramey

Clockwork ticking drew Jakob Adams' eyes to a cherry wood desk, the central feature of Captain Wallace's spacious study. On its polished top, an overturned dragonfly lifted and fell, lifted and fell. The size of a hand, with gemstone eyes and gossamer wings, its features were exquisitely rendered, but the inflexible metal body could not right itself. Jakob debated whether to help or crush the device. *Life is struggle*, he thought. *Succeed or die.*

Footsteps sounded. Jakob turned as an imposing man with fleshy jowls strode in, wide blue eyes sparking with a zealot's fervor. His double-breasted suit was pressed in the military fashion.

"You must be Captain Wallace," Jakob said.

"And you will be Adams." Wallace brushed past him to a padded chair behind the desk. The scent of sandalwood cologne trailed him. He swept the dragonfly into a drawer that muffled but did not extinguish its struggles. "I trust your flight was uneventful."

"It was," Jakob said. "There was so little headwind the dirigible arrived in Pittsburgh an hour early. I took the steam train to New Castle from there."

Wallace rubbed his chins. "I sent a motor carriage for you. Did you not get my message?" He inhaled. "Pulaski!"

Steps staccatoed. A lean man appeared between open pocket doors. "Sir?"

"Send a message to Pittsburgh," Wallace said. "Tell Carlisle to return at once."

"Yes sir." The manservant turned crisply and hurried away.

"Sit," Wallace said. "You must be wondering why I summoned you."

Jakob sat. "Your invitation suggested an offer of employment." He gazed directly into Wallace's face, having long ago broken his father's habit of staring at his betters' shoe tops. Tycoons were men too.

"Cigarette?" Wallace said. A clacking whir sounded beneath the desk. A panel opened. A silver device pushed up, cigarette squeezed between metal protrusions. Another appendage shot forth. Blue flame flared.

"I do not smoke," Jakob said.

Wallace waved the comment away. "Wise. Less chance for explosion." The device retracted, dropping its cigarette onto the desk amid a litter of spilled tobacco grains.

Explosion? Jakob thought.

Wallace shuffled through papers. He leaned from his chair to press a switch on the wall behind him. A buzzing sound ensued, and the room brightened. A tube around the ceiling's perimeter glowed with a greenish cast. Particles streamed through it like a sandstorm, emitting light enough to read by.

"A Geissler tube?" Jakob said. He had no idea which noble gas might produce such an effect.

Wallace glanced up. "My son's design. I'll not go into details. Suffice it to say the lighting for the manor comes from a single source, a passive engine if you will."

"I would be most interested in examining it," Jakob said.

"Why?" Wallace's expression turned suspicious.

Jakob winced. He should have realized that a man with Wallace's wealth would be protective of his inventions. "I am an engineer, sir. That is presumably why you invited me."

Wallace nodded. "It was your stint on Brooklyn's bridge that drew my attention. Specifically, your familiarity with caisson work."

"Caissons?" Jakob was not aware of rivers in the area that might call for deep pilings. Caissons had been utilized in New York because the supports required underwater excavation. Many workers had been afflicted with caisson disease as a result. Even Jakob had been mildly impacted. He would not soon forget the pain that bubbled from his blood.

"I need someone with experience maintaining air flow and pressure under difficult conditions," Wallace said. "Are you my man?"

"That would depend upon the circumstances of my employment."

"Money?"

"That," Jakob said. "And position. I come from humble beginnings." His parents had immigrated to America in 1854 and continued to live in Chicago, where his father worked in the stockyards. It was backbreaking, unappreciated work, the men as expendable as the cattle they carved. "Through initiative and hard work, I have achieved a measure of reputation. I mean to step up from my current position."

"Of course," Wallace said. "This is management I offer, with a term of no less than five years. Your rapid rise at Berlind is one reason I contacted you."

Jakob nodded. He hoped Wallace's background research would not uncover that his rise at the Berlind Bridge Works was due in great measure to the affections of Berlind's wife. She admired his work ethic, particularly when he removed his clothes.

"One hundred a month," Wallace said, "plus a bonus for delivering the first phase on time."

Jakob turned the cigarette like a compass needle seeking north. "I want to inspect the work site and architectural plans. I must assure myself that the endeavor is feasible. Many a rising career has foundered upon the shoals of a rich man's pipedream."

"You need not worry on that account," Wallace said. "The project has been vetted by minds more educated than yours."

"I will make that determination for myself," Jakob said. His gaze went to a golden cufflink on Wallace's sleeve that bore the compass and protractor symbol of the freemasons.

"Do not push me," Wallace said. "You are in no position to bully your way."

Jakob stood from his chair. "Nor do I intend to be bullied."

Wallace blew out a breath. "Oh, very well. My foreman will show you in the morning."

"Agreed," Jakob said. "I'll return after breakfast."

"You will be here by eight AM," Wallace said. "Do not think our future relations will follow tonight's example. I am in charge of every detail of this project and you will follow my orders precisely." His tone conveyed a spring wound tight.

Jakob shrugged. "So long as your orders do not prevent me completing my work, I am content with that arrangement."

Wallace's face reddened until he seemed about to explode. Smiling secretly, Jakob turned and walked out. He had come close to overplaying his hand, but it was worth that chance to restore a modicum of humility to Wallace. His father would lick boots for a chance to work for this man. Jakob would not.

As he passed beneath the glowing tube, the hair on the back of his neck stood erect. A shudder took his shoulders. He imagined hordes of locusts trapped within that glass.

Promptly at eight the next morning, Jakob approached Wallace's house. The air was crisp with a hint of lingering frost. He took a moment to enjoy the view of downtown New Castle in the valley below. Horse carriages navigated brick streets a few blocks from a row of factories belting out streams of black smoke. A locomotive pulled into a gate while coal boats drifted through a canal.

"You like?" A muscular Italian with a bushy mustache stepped down from the wraparound porch. "Smell of the progress, *si*?"

"Yes," Jakob said. He extended his hand. "I am Jakob Adams."

"Anthony," the man said. "Anthony Ricci. You call me Rizzi, *si*?"

"Fine," Jakob said. "Nice to make your acquaintance, Anthony. Will Captain Wallace be joining us?"

"Later maybe," Rizzi said. "Now I show to you drawings."

"Lead on," Jakob said. He couldn't decide whether Wallace slighted him by relegating him to the foreman or showed respect in allowing him to inspect blueprints without supervision.

Rizzi took him down a narrow roadway scraped into the side of the hill. Jakob hadn't even seen a hint of the road on his walk from the hotel in town. The tangled mess of leafless trees and shrubs that dominated the hillside must mask it.

"So, Anthony," Jakob said. "What is this project of Captain Wallace's, exactly?"

Rizzi glanced at him. "You ask him, okay?"

"I ask you. Are you not the foreman?"

"*Si*." Rizzi's head bobbed. "As the fore man, I tell you ask him."

"I am about to become your boss. Are you certain you want us to begin on this sour note?"

Rizzi snorted. "Captain Wallace tell me when you boss."

"Your choice," Jakob said. He pulled his coat tight.

They arrived at a narrow carriage house. Piles of droppings attested to the recent presence of horses. Frozen furrows indicated carts.

"Drawings in there," Rizzi said. He opened the door with a key from his pocket, and motioned Jakob inside. The interior was more comfortably furnished than he would have guessed, with a small, high table and three folding chairs. A fanciful green area rug covered part of the floor. Heat gushed from a square metal device in one corner. Within the confines of its metal grill, Jakob saw a greenish glow and heard a distant buzz. His interest piqued at the thought of a technology that might produce light as well as heat, but Rizzi was already unrolling a chart across the table. The drawing depicted a tunnel running northeast. Smaller branches were only rudimentarily shown.

"A mine?" Jakob said. "Why would Wallace want my help with that?" He'd never set foot in a mine.

"He tell me show drawings." Rizzi indicated the page before Jakob.

"Where is this tunnel, geographically?"

"Is close."

"You're as cryptic as Wallace," Jakob said. "If I'm to be the project manager, do you not think it would be in everyone's interest to appraise me of significant details?"

"*Si.*" Rizzi unrolled a second chart, a cutaway view of the tunnel with callout details for the support beams.

"This shows me nothing useful," Jakob said.

Rizzi unrolled a final chart depicting a side view of a tunnel plunging downward at steep angle.

"A deep shaft, then," Jakob said. "Is there water? Is the tunnel flooded? Is that why Wallace thinks he needs caissons?" Surely better methods existed to deal with that situation.

"I show you drawings," Rizzi said. "*Si?*"

"I may just make it my first duty to fire you, Rizzi."

"You no fire me. I Captain Wallace's favorite. I rescue his son."

"From what?" Jakob said.

"You finish here?" Rizzi rolled the charts and set them aside. "You want I show you tunnel?"

Jakob frowned. "A minute ago you wouldn't even divulge where it was."

Rizzi chortled as if that were the best joke he'd heard. He kicked the rug so that a portion of it folded back upon itself. Beneath, was the unmistakable outline of a hatch.

"Under you feet." Rizzi showed a gap-toothed grin. "You not suspect, *si?*"

"Not only did I not suspect," Jakob said, "I don't see the purpose."

Rizzi lifted the hatch via a ring inset into its surface. The buzzing sound intensified. A simple ladder led down. Rizzi descended.

Jakob hesitated. Whispers nipped at his thoughts. The closeness of the opening reminded him of a caisson. There was no peace in those concrete tombs thirty feet below the river surface. He'd had nightmares throughout his stint on the Brooklyn bridge.

"You coming?" Rizzi said.

"Yes." Jakob had not let Brooklyn stop him and would not let this mine do it either. He took a deep breath and started down, counting rungs to keep his thoughts occupied. His foot struck solid ground after the fifteenth.

"You gonna have to climb faster, you work here," Rizzi said.

The dark seemed to squeeze around Jakob. The steady buzz enveloped him. There was an ebb and flow to the sound, a pulse that quickly transformed in his mind to the chugging of air pumps, the jostling of men working past one another, the clank of their pick or shovel striking rock. A sewage smell wafted. His gorge slammed up his throat. He retched, bending hands on knees.

Rizzi clasped his shoulder. "You okay?"

"Fine," Jakob managed. He swallowed.

"You wanna go back?"

"No," Jakob said. It was not real, none of it was real. He had left Brooklyn behind. He squeezed his eyes closed and forced his thoughts to happier places, the dirigible floating over endless forest, champagne bubbling in his mouth. That was what he wanted, not the bridge, not the black muck that seeped through seals and coated everything with its stink.

Rizzi pulled a lever. The tunnel flooded with greenish light. To one side, a square device no higher than Jakob's thigh hummed loudly. Two tubes extended upward from the device—which must surely be the passive engine Wallace had mentioned—and bent along the ceiling, down the tunnel. Jakob stared past support beam after support beam until the tunnel dipped out of sight.

Opposite the passive engine, a low-ceilinged chamber held stacks of wooden beams, coiled ropes, and assorted bags.

"How did you get those beams down here?" Jakob said.

Rizzi shrugged. "Tunnel already here. We build carriage house above."

Jakob could understand that Wallace might want to hide his efforts to mine beneath his house, but why go to so much trouble to disguise an existing mine? Surely there must be records of it.

Rizzi led Jakob past a line of ore cars. Narrow rail tracks ran down both sides of the tunnel.

"Here," Rizzi said. He opened a door inscribed into the side of the foremost car. A panel lit with the same greenish glow. Rizzi sat on a bench, facing it. Jakob perched upon a second small bench behind him.

The car rolled forward. Unable to see through Rizzi's broad shoulders, Jakob settled for watching the tunnel wall slide past. Smaller tunnels intersected the main one. Some were barely crevices, a few were more substantial. These were filled with construction rubble.

Movement caught Jakob's eye. A small creature reared atop a heap of broken bricks, pointed nose sniffing. A greenish glow emitted from its flesh. The car rolled past, and it was gone.

He nudged Rizzi. "What was that?"

Rizzi craned his neck. "What you mean?"

"That animal in the side tunnel? Did you see it?"

Rizzi shrugged. "Sewer rat. Tunnels full of them."

"But it... glowed."

Rizzi shrugged again.

"Should we capture it?" Jakob said. "The mechanism of its glow might advance our science."

Rizzi laughed. "Sure, boss. You go catch it your bare hands, *si*? Take it back. They tell you sewer rat."

The descent abruptly steepened. The car picked up speed. Side tunnels became less frequent, then absent. Something had changed about the main tunnel too. It took a few seconds for Jakob to realize what.

"Where are the supports?" They descended through solid rock, through an oval corridor with walls so smooth they appeared to be hand chiseled. "How is this possible?"

"I tell you," Rizzi said. "Tunnel already here."

"That doesn't tell me anything. Who constructed it? When? Why?"

"Ask God," Rizzi said. They came to a level section. The car slowed to a stop in a chamber crammed with supplies, including a few picks and shovels and candle hats. They must be approaching the active work site. The track curved in a tight circle such that the car could return up the opposite side.

Rizzi opened the door. Jakob climbed out. "Where is everyone?" he said.

"Come again?"

"The workers? There are no workers."

"Captain Wallace send them away until problem fixed."

"What problem?"

"Your problem."

"Caissons? I haven't seen a dribble of water. If I am to solve Wallace's problem, I must know what it is."

Rizzi nodded. One corner of his mouth sucked in. He came to a decision. "You come," he said. "I show you. You no tell Captain Wallace, *si?*"

"I won't tell," Jakob said. *Finally.*

Rizzi led him down a shallower incline. The light tube did not extend here, but enough light remained by which to navigate. While the tunnel's smooth bore continued, there was evidence of pick marks on the floor, and small piles of stone chip rubble.

"Problem there," Rizzi said, pointing to a barrier in the tunnel ahead. Boards had been nailed haphazardly to obstruct the way forward.

"Why is it blocked?"

"Bad gas."

"And Wallace thinks a caisson is the answer."

Rizzi shrugged.

Jakob peered between boards. In the distance, he thought he could make out a greenish glow, but it was difficult to be certain.

A grunt came from the darkness. Jakob froze, ears straining. A second grunt sounded.

"Is someone there?" he said. He yanked at the outermost board. "Do you need help?"

"No." Rizzi pulled Jakob away and inserted himself between Jacob and the barrier. "Is all right. You imagine."

"Is it gas?" Jakob sniffed. The air was dank, but he smelled nothing unusual.

"*Si,*" Rizzi said. "Gas." He tapped his temple. "You brain, it confused here."

"What is the source of the—"

An arm shot between boards. The elbow wrapped Rizzi's neck and slammed his head to the barrier. The skin of the arm glowed vaguely green. Rizzi reached out. His face darkened. His eyes bulged.

Move, Jakob thought. *Help him.* He had witnessed a man drown in Brooklyn. An air pump had failed. Others frantically tried to start the backup pumps, but Jakob could only watch as the water seeped up the man's corded neck, around his face, into his screaming mouth. He still heard echoes of that scream in his nightmares.

A gurgle sputtered from Rizzi's mouth.

"No!" Jakob shouted. He'd not watch death again. He surged forward and grabbed at the arm. The flesh was rubbery. His hands slipped. Blood welled slowly from scrapes in that alien arm. Jakob wedged his feet at the base of the barrier and tried again.

Like a rust-frozen hinge, the elbow slowly straightened. A grunt sounded and the arm pulled back through the boards. Rizzi sagged forward.

Jakob eased the larger man to the floor. There was no light behind the barricade now, no greenish glow, only the utter blackness of an unlit tunnel.

"*Grazie*," Rizzi gasped. "*Grazie*."

"What... who was that?" Jakob said. His heart thudded. Jakob helped Rizzi to his feet.

"Is nothing," Rizzi said. He brushed his pants and walked toward the ore car. "You no tell Captain Wallace I bring you this place, *si*?"

"Tell *me*, Anthony. Explain what I witnessed, and I will have no need to inquire it of Wallace."

Rizzi tapped his temple. "Gas."

"That was no hallucination," Jakob said. He rubbed his hands together. He could still feel the unnatural chill of the creature.

"You come," Rizzi said. "Captain Wallace not patient." He opened the car's door. Jakob picked a shred of skin from beneath his fingernail. It was pale white, entirely ordinary. *Was* the experience mere illusion, a waking dream facilitated by his experience in the caissons? He walked to the car and sat on the back bench. Rizzi resumed his seat. The panel lit.

Jakob inspected his fingernails as the car began its climb. There was no evidence, no greenish glow, just that shred of perfectly normal skin. For all he knew, he had scratched Rizzi.

The buzz suddenly intruded into his thoughts. It was everywhere, a colony of bees swarming. The hair on his arms lifted. He leaned into the car's side, away from the wall.

There was no sign of the glowing rat. Maybe he had imagined that too. Gases *were* known to impart odd effects. It had seemed so real. Fear pushed at him. Curiosity pulled back. If psychic phenomenon was a property of some new gas, the man to harvest that power might become as wealthy as Captain Wallace.

The car finally slowed to a stop beneath the carriage house. Rizzi exited as if nothing unusual had happened.

"I cannot ignore this," Jakob said. "I must know more if I am to accept this position."

"Go some other job," Rizzi said, "some other place."

"Why?" Jakob said. "I regret that we got off on the wrong foot, Riz... Anthony. I am a decent fellow. I shall treat you and the workers right."

"You go," Rizzi said. "Live happy life, have lotsa kids."

"Tell me," Jakob said. "You know what's happening down there. I know you do."

"Ask God," Rizzi said. He started up the ladder.

"You can trust me," Jakob said. "My parents came to this country from Poland without a penny in their pockets. I have worked hard to make a better life. Just like you, Anthony."

The hatch opened. Jakob climbed after the Italian. Rizzi was putting away the drawings when Jakob emerged.

"You gotta wife, Mister Adam? You gotta children?"

"No," Jakob said.

"Then you no like me, understand? I come this country Dominico Ricci. They change my name Tony because I going 'To NY' and Rizzi because their tongues *al dente*, no speak it right. This best job I find. I leave someday. Now I gotta stay for wife, gotta stay for sons and daughter. You no gotta stay. You no wanna end up down there, understand?" He made a gesture toward the tunnel.

Jakob stared blankly. What could he say to that?

"You right," Rizzi said. "Was real down there. Is gas, like I say. It... change things. You go, *si*? Leave the New Castle. No see Captain Wallace, no take job."

"Is Wallace conducting some sort of experiment?"

Rizzi shook his head. "Captain Wallace want it pushed outta there. He no want workers hurt. He want the glow dust, not the gas. He want the light."

"Ah," Jakob said. "He hopes to use a positive pressure caisson to keep the gas out. I see now." They were mining fuel for Wallace's passive engines.

Rizzi closed the hatch and replaced the rug. "You no see, Mr. Adam. Hear. Listen Dominco Ricci. Be wise, my friend. I say to Wallace you never arrive this morning."

"Thank you," Jakob said.

"*Eccellente, il mio amico!*" Rizzi's mustaches lifted. He clapped Jakob's shoulder and shoved him toward the glowing grate. "Warm youself. I go back. You close door when you leave, *si*? Is already locked."

Jakob nodded, eyeing the rolled charts Rizzi had replaced on a narrow shelf. Perhaps there were other charts too.

"Good morning Adams," Wallace said as Jakob entered the study. The dragonfly had been replaced with a bronze crocodile paperweight. Wallace nodded to the manservant, who bowed and slid the pocket doors closed. "That fool, Rizzi, babbled something about you not showing up. Did he miss you?"

"No," Jakob said. "As a matter of fact, he showed me everything."

"What does that mean? He was told to show you the blueprints and the tunnel. What more--"

"You're mining ore for your passive engines. You hope to find a stronger vein."

"Rizzi told you this?"

"I deduced it. The green tint in your light tube, the similar glow in the tunnel. It's the only thing that makes sense."

"Let us say you are correct," Wallace said. "You do see the potential of such a find, do you not?"

"I do," Jakob said. "But there is another thing I know."

Wallace's eyebrow lifted.

"I know about the odorless gas that transforms animals—and people, apparently—into something other than themselves."

Wallace leaned back. Calculation clouded his gaze. He sighed. "Go on."

"I also know what will happen should the authorities learn of this."

"Do you, now?"

"It came to me on my walk from the carriage house. Why undertake such an elaborate means to hide the shaft if not to elude prosecution? I believe I could see you clapped in irons with a few carefully chosen words."

Wallace laughed. "Believe again, Adams. Every sheriff and judge between here and Pittsburgh are in my pocket. I doubt you could find a sympathetic ear." He yawned. "I hide the tunnel because it is in my interest to hide it. Now, tell me what you want before I have you prosecuted for trespass."

"A seat on the board," Jakob said. "A stake in the company."

"Partnership?" Wallace clapped his hands. "You want *partnership* in my project?"

Jakob nodded. "I want your assurance, in writing, that such a path is open to me."

Wallace's face puffed. "How dare you demand anything. I can have you crushed with a single edict, your family killed, everything you prize destroyed. The countryside is littered with unnamed immigrant graves. Do not forget that."

Anger flared through Jakob. He started to stand.

"Oh, sit down," Wallace said. His hand slipped below the desktop. A drawer slid open. Jakob prepared to dodge a bullet.

Instead, Wallace placed a stack of papers onto the desk and tapped them into alignment. "I have every intention of rewarding you for your work, Adams. I take care of my own. Deliver the first stage on time and on budget and this agreement grants you a one percent—"

"Five."

"One," Wallace said. "If this project delivers as I anticipate, even one percent will make you rich."

"In that case," Jakob said, "you can surely offer three."

Wallace chuckled. "You do have spunk, Adams." He rubbed his face. "Deliver the first phase for one percent. Upon completion of the final phase, I shall have the agreement redrafted to raise it to three. Do we have a deal?" He slid the stack across and offered a pen. Ink glistened from the Nib.

Jakob set the top page aside.

"Don't bother to read it," Wallace said. "It is as unfair to you as you can possibly imagine. While engaged on the project, you belong to me, you will live where I say to live, eat what I say to eat, work the hours I decree. No fraternizing, no going into town to slake your thirst in the company of other immigrant souls, only work and more work. By the time this is finished, you will have spent so much time underground that you will no longer know what natural light is." He pressed the pen into Jakob's fingers. "In return, I shall make you rich, Adams. That is the deal, take it or leave it."

"What does this 'first phase' consist of?" Jakob said.

Wallace waved dismissively. "Proof of concept at scale. My son has an idea. I want it engineered and developed into a working prototype. The first phase ends with successful deployment of a sleeve."

Jakob opened his mouth.

"Do not worry," Wallace said. "There is plenty of time built into the agreement for construction and testing. If you are half the engineer your resume implies, you will finish a month before the deadline."

"And I am to take your word on that?" Jakob said.

"You are." The determined set of Wallace's eyes told Jakob all he needed to know about further negotiation. He scratched his name onto the agreement with a flourish.

Wallace nodded energetically. "Welcome to the project, Mister Adams. My son calls it The Glow. Imagine, Adams. Entire city blocks lit by our light, factories powered by our engines, every mansion in town, your mansion, heated with our heaters, cooled by our fans. We will be kings."

He reached across the desk and took Jakob's hand into his iron grip. Jakob thought of the arm lunging around Rizzi, the rubbery texture of the creature's skin. The sewer rat. *You no wanna end up down there, understand?* He might have signed his death warrant by accepting Wallace's offer. Still, one percent stake with a potential for three? It was far better than Jakob could have anticipated. If he meant to become one of the elite he may as well get used to the price of admission.

Wallace released. The Masonic ring on his finger glinted.

My Brother's Keeper

Lavonne Lyles

Am I my brother's keeper? Should teardrops fill my eyes?
His body just expired, in the woods beneath the skies.
No one showed him pity, no one eased his pain.
Shall he ever be forsaken, he who lives out in the rain.
Is there no compassion, is there no remorse?
Am I my brother's keeper? I let him die, of course.

Deja vu Pow Wow

Jere Moon

Drums sounded. Mother Earth's heartbeat. The Pow Wow was about to begin.

My friend, Raegan, pointed to the back row of New Castle's mini-amphitheater located on East Washington Street at Riverside Park. "Debbie, there's two spots."

We had attended concerts and other events here, but never a Pow Wow. Holding tightly to our vanilla lattes that we had just purchased at the Confluence next door, we squeezed in between people already seated on the smooth stones. Water trickled from the fountain to our right. Neshannock Creek babbled behind us.

"It's the perfect location," I said. "In the mid 1700s, New Castle was the capital of the Lenni Lenape Tribe. Neshannock, place of two streams, stems from the Lenape word nisha, meaning two. The Neshannock is a tributary of the Shenango River. Both meet here in our little town."

Raegan yawned. "Put your research for your historical romance novel to sleep and kick back and enjoy."

I took a sip of coffee. "I'll try."

The Master of Ceremonies greeted the audience and announced there would be a contest for best dancers and traditional dress. Each contestant was introduced as he or she entered the open air patio. Their tribal regalia showcased intricate bead-work and feather creations. Attire as well as dancing would be judged.

I smiled as a Native American man with coal black hair introduced as Anoki, strutted a primitive breech clout, a breastplate made of deer tibia bones, and a pair of fringed leather moccasins.

"I'm voting for him," Reagan said. "He's handsome!"

"Anoki's dressed like a Woodland Native American before contact and influence with European traders," I said. "I'm writing about them."

Reagan just shook her head.

I took another sip of coffee. "Sorry. I've had writer's block lately. I'm hoping this Pow Wow snaps me out of it."

"I do too," she said. "I can't wait until you get that book published, it's all you talk about."

The youngest in the contest was a dark-haired baby girl fastened inside a cradleboard decorated with beaded geometric designs. Strapped to her mother's back, she seemed perfectly content to be part of the ritual. An elderly man with a long, white braid and a serious limp, entered last, but he kept up with pace.

The first number was a two-step that involved all contestants. Next, the men performed a hunting dance. Holding spear or bow, they shielded their eyes from the sun and crept about as if looking for wildlife. When the song ended, Anoki held up a stuffed toy turkey to signify a successful hunt. Everyone cheered.

The blanket dance followed. Each woman displayed a colorful woven blanket folded over her arm as she took slow pristine steps around the dance area.

Younger contestants entered the Fancy Dance recognized by its flashy clothing. Females in leather dresses twirled colorful shawls around their bodies, while they spun around doing a light-footed stomp. Young men wearing eagle feather bustles and horsehair streamers over rawhide leggings and breech clouts, performed precise steps punctuated by loud drumbeats.

Next, came the courting dance. The women joined hands and formed a circle around the men. In the center, each man took a turn whooping and hollering while he performed athletic feats to impress a particular maiden. Anoki's breech clout flapped in the breeze as he executed twirling leaps. Was he looking at me?

Raegan broke my reverie. "Let's check out the vendors and get something to eat."

"Yeah. Yeah. Sure." Even though the song wasn't over, I stood and followed my friend to the back of the amphitheater where a railing separated us from the creek. The flowing green water had been blessed earlier by one of the elders during a quiet ceremony that offered tobacco smoke to the Creator. Now with drums pounding, the place took on new meaning. As I looked at ducks, I envisioned canoes of natives paddling downstream to attend today's gathering.

Raegan pulled my arm and led me to East Washington Street that had been blocked off and lined with booths of Native American crafts, everything from beaded jewelry to woven rugs. We went inside the first tent.

"Porcupine quill earrings," Raegan said. "Imagine making those."

"Native Americans didn't waste anything," I said.

What caught my eye was a sleek, cream-colored, ankle length, doeskin dress with fringe on the underarms.

"This is just like the dress in my novel that Doe Eyes' Indian mother gave her to wear when she was taken captive by the Lenapes and adopted into their tribe. It would be fun to wear to my book signings."

"Buy it," Raegan said.

I peeked at the price tag. "Six hundred dollars!" I backed away.

"Whoa, that's steep," Raegan said.

The shop's owner, a matronly Native American woman, rushed over, removed the dress from its hanger, and held it to my shoulders. "It is expensive because it's made of four deer skins, not two. They were brain-tanned by my son. Feel."

I ran my palm across the soft nap. "I wish . . ."

The woman brought the dress over my head and pulled it down into place. Even over my tee-shirt and jeans, it fit like it was made for me.

I twirled, transformed, no longer a 21st century, white American woman with a job, bills, and errands to run. The sound of the drums moved me. Ancient visualizations .

"Wow!" Raegan said. "You look great. You just need to braid your hair." The woman nodded. Raegan transformed my long hair.

A voice rattled over the loudspeaker. "The dancers are entering the audience to look for a partner."

Raegan looked over my shoulder. Her cheeks reddened.

"What?" I said. "Do I have food on my face?"

Someone tapped my shoulder.

I turned.

Anoki towered over me in his skimpy breech clout. He clasped my hand in his and led me toward the dance area.

I glanced back at the woman.

She motioned me to go.

Raegan winked.

It was a warm September day, but I felt cool and comfortable in the deerskin garment a I imitated the two-step. As the rhythm increased, I became Doe Eyes, dancing the Harvest dance at the Lenape village. Never before had I felt so alive, the wind in my hair, the sun on my back. The crowd cheered just as they did in my novel.

The song ended much too soon. I could have danced all day. The Master of Ceremonies announced there would be a short intermission while the judges determined the winners.

During the break, Anoki told me he was a professional Pow Wow dancer from out west. He competed in Pow Wows all over the country. The prize money, often a substantial amount, provided a comfortable living and enabled him to keep his heritage alive.

I stood captivated as he told the tale of the four deer I was wearing.

"They gave up their lives during archery season in Montana. Every deer's brain contains enough oils to tan the width and length of its pelt. My mother spent weeks hand stitching the hides together into this beautiful dress."

I was lost in Anoki's gorgeous hazel eyes and almost missed the connection. "She's your mother—the woman who made this?"

Anoki nodded.

Drums sounded.

"That's our signal to return."

Don't go, I thought. I want to be Doe Eyes for just a little longer.

But that was not to be. I followed Anoki back to the arena.

A crowd gathered.

Anoki was announced most agile dancer. I applauded. He deserved it.

"And the winner of the most beautiful dress," the M.C. said. "Anoki's final partner."

That's nice, I thought.

Anoki gestured toward me. "That's you."

"Me?"

"Let's go get our prizes." Anoki pulled me in front of the audience.

He won two hundred dollars. I was speechless as the M.C. put six bills in my hand.

"The judges know quality when they see it," Anoki said.

"True, but this belongs to your mother."

I ran back to the vendor area and presented her with the prize money. Carefully, I took off the dress. "Thank-you for a once in a lifetime opportunity."

She put the cash in her pocket and pushed the doeskin masterpiece toward me. "It's yours now. You paid for it."

"Are you sure?"

She nodded.

I hugged her. "Thank you. You don't know what this means to me."

"I think I do know, Doe Eyes."

Doe Eyes? My ears rang. My body tingled.

Raegan approached with a grin. "Wow! You looked like a natural out there."

I introduced her to Anoki. He invited us to lunch.

We walked to the food court. The scent of roasting meat and fresh bread made my mouth water. I wasn't sure what was on the menu, but I knew it wasn't your typical fair food.

Raegan had a buffalo burger. Anoki and I had chili and fry bread. The chili consisted of fresh tomatoes, corn, beans, onions, a mixture of beef and buffalo, seasoned with just the right amount of chili peppers and cumin. The fry bread was light and puffy, fried a golden brown. It complemented the chili perfectly.

"It's delicious," I said. "Every bite makes my mouth water for more."

Anoki smiled. "I'm glad you like it. It is unique to our tribe and was prepared by our elders."

Raegan snickered as I scraped the bowl and licked the spoon.

"Where are you heading next?" she asked Anoki.

He picked up his bow and stood. "The Red River Pow Wow in Pittsburgh."

Raegan checked her phone map. "That's about an hour away. Did Debbie tell you she's writing a Native American novel? You'd look perfect on the cover."

I felt my cheeks flush. "Raegan!"

"It's okay," Anoki said. "I would be honored." He held up his bow and posed.

When the Pow Wow ended, Anoki and I exchanged business cards and vowed to stay in touch. Raegan and I waved good-bye and got into my Rav4 to go home.

I turned the key in the ignition and looked into my rear view mirror so I could back out of my parking space. My heart pounded when I saw Anoki sprinting toward my car. I quickly put it in park and lowered the driver's side window.

"I just remembered something," he said breathlessly. "The Red River Pow Wow in Pittsburgh has a couples competition. I think you and I should enter. The prize is a $1,000." He met my gaze and lingered. "Is it a date?"

I couldn't speak, but nodded yes.

"Great. I've got your number. I'll call you soon." He disappeared toward his car.

I glanced at Raegan. "Am I dreaming?"

A beep from my computer sounded. I opened my eyes and lifted my head off my keyboard.

I wasn't at a Pow Wow. I was in my writing room. Alone.

It had been a dream. A beautiful dream that ended my writer's block. I started typing.

Drums sounded. The Pow Wow was about to begin.

INDIAN FRY BREAD

4 CUPS FLOUR
1 CUP WATER
2 ¼ TEASPOONS BAKING POWDER
PINCH SALT
OIL

Mix together flour, water, baking powder and salt until well-blended. Kneed one minute. Cover and let rise 15-20 minutes. Pat dough out ½ inch thick. Cut in wedges. Make a 1-inch slit in middle of each wedge. Heat 1 ½ inches of oil in large skillet. Fry wedges until golden brown.

Born a Psychic Medium

Kat Rodgers

Cindy Burkett Willoughby, a local psychic medium, lives and works on the North Hill of New Castle. Her journey began steeped in spiritual intrigue on her unique birth night.

The year was 1974, a Friday the thirteenth. The mysterious sky over New Castle, Pennsylvania cast a divine air of mysticism. Stars twinkled brightly in December's dark new moon phase as a partial eclipse of the sun and a meteor shower occurred.

Inside St. Francis Hospital, Mrs. Burkett clenched her teeth and pushed with all her might. She unleashed a painful birthing scream. A baby's cry filled the room as a mother, in joyful exhaustion, sank against pillows while nurses cleaned and tended to the infant. Sister Carolyn dimmed the bright lights above the patient's bed as Sister Agnes gently placed the swaddled newborn into the crook of a parent's awaiting arm.

"Does she have a name?" Sister Agnes asked. "This one is a special gift. God's blessing!"

Sister Carolyn straightened her black tunic. "And this day is quite godly." With a sigh, she clutched Rosary beads in her palm. "Today is a Holy Day. It's St. Lucy's Day, also known as St. Lucia's Day! How about the birth name Lucy or Lucia?"

"Thank you, Sister Agnes," replied the proud father, Vince, from the sidelines. "But I have already picked out a name. Cindy."

Sister Agnes tilted her head in thought. "I do believe it's of Greek origin and means 'moon goddess' or 'moon' even though it can't be seen in the sky tonight. It's actually a 'new moon.' And, this is the season of advent that leads to Christmas Day, the birth of Jesus. Her birthday will always be surrounded in religion."

"We'll be back in twenty minutes to take her to the nursery," Sister Agnes said. She marked the infant's forehead with the sign of the cross and a kiss. "I promise you'll get her back at dawn's light for breast feeding." She gazed at the baby. "Precious! Lest you forget, extraordinary mystical forces of nature escorted this soul into this world tonight."

The nuns exchanged glances and a hand gesture. Sister Agnes drew the curtains wide. "The Geminid meteor shower happens on this day, every year."

Sister Carolyn crossed her palms over her chest. "Such a wondrous cosmic event. There's a natural fireworks show of shooting stars going on! We are on our way to the upper balcony to watch. Would you care to join us, Mr. Burkett?"

Both nuns hurried out of the room.

When Cindy was four years old, her mother left, never to return. This child was raised by her father and grandparents. As Cindy grew up, her single obstacle in life was larger than not having her mother around. It stemmed from the realization that she was totally alone with the spirits she saw, heard, and talked to.

Such was a day when Cindy clung to her grandmother's hand as they leisurely strolled along the shopping district downtown New Castle. A lady wearing a wide-brimmed hat and scarlet dress stood in a second floor store window waving. On tiptoes, Cindy swayed one arm in the air as the other tugged on the hem of her granny's floral skirt.

"Who are you waving to?" Cindy's grandmother asked.

Cindy pointed. "That pretty lady in red."

"I don't see her. It's just your imagination."

"Nuh-uh. Look, she's right there!"

As Cindy grew, incidents such as that one left her with many unanswered questions, thoughts, and emotions. She felt isolated with the voices she heard and the people she saw every day and night.

Never having experienced death, Cindy didn't know she was 'talking to the dead'. Telepathically, she communicated with them but learned to keep it her secret.

It wasn't until Cindy, a teenager, was in the middle of the grocery store by herself when an unknown woman touched her elbow. The lady gazed into Cindy's chocolate eyes fringed in heavy lashes and softly said, "Little girl, do you sometimes think you are CRAZY?"

Cindy's shy nod and leveled eyes encouraged the lady to continue. "Not at all. You're a psychic medium like me. We talk to the dead to help the family and friends left behind. You and I were born with a gift from God!"

"My grandma says it's all in my mind."

"Not everybody has or understands our abilities. It will drive you bonkers if you don't know how to turn it on and off. I will help you."

That exchange redirected Cindy's path and journey. For the very first time in her life, Cindy was not alone in her experiences with spirits. When she got home she told her great-grandmother about the incident. To her surprise, Cindy discovered that this relative saw spirits but didn't dare talk about it. But this day she did, out of a need to offer Cindy added comfort and calm any fears. Nevertheless, certain images and spirits occasionally terrified her throughout childhood.

Ghost Hunters debuted on television in 2004 when Cindy turned twenty. She became a fan of the series and gained insight to some of her experiences. Cindy began her own research and landed a job as case manager for the Greater Pittsburgh Paranormal Society. There, she once again crossed paths with the helpful lady she had encountered at the market years prior.

In 2005, a supernatural drama TV show, *Medium*, came into the public eye. Cindy learned how to apply her unique ability, her birthright, to serve the Spirit World.

Cindy was able to stop hiding and embraced her gift. She began with private readings for those wishing to communicate with departed loved ones. Cindy helped others find closure and guided them in their own spiritual paths. Word-of-mouth spread around town. She knew it was meant to be.

"The dead are not gone forever," Cindy said, "They are simply in another place that we all will reach at the end of our lives."

A medium is like a blank canvas is to an artist. Whether spirits talk about the past, present, or future, Cindy verbally paints a precise 'spiritual image' for clients through a spirit's words, messages, gestures, and spiritual symbols throughout the sitting. This provides evidence that she genuinely connected with the client's loved ones.

Occasionally, the readings produce a less detailed 'glimpse' when spirits simply want to show their presence for the sake of comfort, peace, and validation.

In 2010, Cindy hung her shingle as a PSYCHIC MEDIUM and independently works from home, by appointment, on Highland Ave., New Castle. She offers private, group, phone, and gallery readings. Cindy's reputation has grown both locally and internationally as a consulted psychic reader and speaker.

Contact her on Facebook, "Readings by Cindy," text, www.CindyPsychicMedium.com, mediumwilloughby@gmail.com, or 724-761-2901.
Photos courtesy of Cindy Burkett Willoughby

The Last Day of School

David L. Withers

Come on! Why is this the longest twenty minutes of school, I think while sitting at my desk in my homeroom. So, I continue to stare up at the large, institutional clock hanging on the wall above the door. It's five after nine o'clock in the morning, June 3, 1965—the last day of school.

It seems like a punishment to have to get up early, shower, get dressed in my usual school clothes. You know, plaid button-down dress shirt, casual pants (no jeans allowed), and black leather shoes. Shirttails tucked in and hair combed, well what hair I have that is long enough to comb. All this effort just to catch the bus, go to my homeroom, wait to be handed my report card, and then to go back to my bus and sent home.

But everyone is excited and happy. Of course they are. It's the start of summer vacation. In a kid's world, this is the second most anticipated day of the year, only following Christmas. Thanksgiving comes in third since you have four days off and it's the kickoff of the holiday season. Halloween is next, dressing up and getting free candy of all kinds. My favorite was Lunch Bars. Then Easter, more candy, the Fourth of July, and maybe Valentine's Day. Labor Day is the worst holiday since it's the start of a whole new school year.

But what also makes the last day of school special is going to Cascade Park for the day. I wish we could go there instead of coming to school, but that's the tradition, or torture.

At last, Miss Hunt is passing out report cards and the yellow buses are lined up in front of the school. I'm so ready to run out of the room, but we have to wait for our group to be called. "Bus 22 can go." I get up and walk across the nearly empty classroom, no books, papers or pencils to carry home, well, except this report card. The room has a strange brightness to it since there are no lessons, artwork, or posters on the walls. I leave it behind, head down the stairs and out the front doors to my bus.

John, my bus driver, is sitting in the driver's seat reading his farm magazine, waiting for us to get settled and seated. He looks up at the large rearview mirror as he pulls the doors shut and shouts, "Come on, the sooner you kids sit down, the sooner we can leave." I sit in the second seat back next to the window like usual. Keith, my buddy sits next to me and we start planning our park adventure. What time are you getting there? Where do you want to meet? What rides do you want to do first?

Keith says, "This year is special because I'll be turning 11 in August and my mother, me, and Roger can go on our own. I don't have to stay with my sister and girl cousins."

Once I get home, I toss my report card on the dining room table and head straight upstairs to my room. I'm so excited about going to the park that I'm out of my school clothes and into my play clothes of jeans, striped tee–shirt and high-top–tennis shoes. I head back down the stairs to the kitchen where my mother is getting ready to make fried egg sandwiches. She already has the potato salad and coleslaw made and stored in Tupperware bowls in the refrigerator.

"I'm ready to go to the park," I say. "What do you want me to put in the car?" I look in the refrigerator for the milk carton.

"What?" my mother says, "We're not leaving for an hour yet. Besides, the park rides don't open until noon."

Great. More waiting! I'm disappointed that I still can't get to the park as the day fades away. A day I've been counting down to since Easter. The last day of school! I sit at the table and slump with my head in my hand and elbows. But the heavy smell of eggs frying in bacon fat makes me realize I am getting a little hungry.

"Tell you what," my mother says while piling eggs on slices of bread, "why don't you make the lemonade. The Kool-Aid packets are in the cupboard." So I get out the Coleman thermos, a couple of ice trays from the freezer, the jar of sugar, and Kool-Aid packets and set them on the counter by the sink.

It does keep me busy so that the time passes before I know it. How did my mother know that would happen? She comes over and says, "Let me taste it." She takes a sip. "Oh my gosh, how much sugar did you put in?" She makes a sour face. "Put some more ice in the thermos, it will probably melt enough by the time we are ready to eat. Let's load up the car."

We have two cardboard boxes packed with food, paper plates and Dixie cups. I carry one out to the car while my mother does the other. And my sister does nothing.

"Now that should stay put and be okay." Mom says as she slams the trunk lid down on our mint green '62 Bel Aire. I jump in the back and slide across the green vinyl seat while my sister sits in front. My mother puts the Chevy in gear and we head out the driveway. *Finally!*

Even though Cascade Park is only about six miles from our farm, it seems like forever to get there. As we drive up Washington Street, I see the old entrance and the midway. We rumble over the bridge that crosses Big Run. Next is the mini–golf course and the iron and neon sign that spans the entrance to the parking lot. Our car gargles over the gravel as Mom looks for a parking spot near the trees.

"Roll the windows down, so the car doesn't get too hot," she tells us. "And look for your aunt and cousins."

"There they are!" I say, pointing to a car parked a couple rows over. They're already walking toward us. With our stuff unloaded and each of us loaded up with our supplies, we head down the tree–lined path to the picnic area. Despite the late start, we're able to find a wooden picnic table under a covered area. It's near the roller coaster tracks and at the edge of the creek. Mom and my aunt start to lay out the tablecloth and set out containers of food, each commenting on what they made. It seems to take forever!

Once they have the paper plates and cups set out, me and my cousins fill up our plates with coleslaw, potato salad, deviled eggs, and sandwiches. The lemonade is still too sweet, but no one seem to mind. Soon my sister and older cousin, Geraldine, head off to find their high school friends, while me and Debbie, my younger cousin, have to stay with our moms while they cover the food up, clean the table, and put the paper plates and cups in the green trash barrels, which are just old 55–gallon drums. By now, the roller coaster has done its first run over the tracks, which means the rides are starting to open.

With our picnic supplies covered up with the tablecloth to keep the flies off the food, we finally start up the midway. I see Keith waiting at the arcade. I tell mom, "There's Keith." She hands me $1.50 for tickets, at 10 cents a ride. That's 15 rides! And she tells me to meet them back at the fountain at the bottom of the midway in an hour and half. Great! Without waiting for her to finish I am gone.

Keith and I wait anxiously for Roger. Within a few minutes, he is walking toward us with a paper cone full of French fries covered in salt and vinegar. What is he doing still eating? Keith and I grab a couple of fries from him and we all head up the hill to the ticket booth near the Ferris wheel. I hand over my $1.50 and get 15 tickets that I roll up and stuff in my jeans

pocket. The three of us go to the Ferris wheel first since there are only a few kids in line.

We get into one car. It's a great way to see more of the park from the higher viewpoint of the wheel. I also think it's cool that we're riding next to an oak tree as high as the Ferris wheel. It seems like you are up in the tree, then falling back down to the ground.

We decide to head across the way to the Tumble Bug. After only a few minutes in line, we zigzag down the wooden ramp to the operator who takes our tickets and lets us onto the platform. We head for the end car and slide around on the wooden seat. Two other kids get in, which fills the car. The operator walks up and fastens the little chain across the opening. That's for keeping us in the car. We grab on to the center iron ring as the ride starts. Since our car isn't crowded, it gives us room to slide around the seat as it circles the track over dips and hills.

Next, we head up the hill to the Merry-go-Round. I'm not a fan of it, and tell Roger and Keith to go ahead, I'll wait this one out. I tell them it's for little kids and moms, and sure enough there's my aunt, mother and little cousin sitting in the Swan-like bench seat. But the truth is, it always makes me sick. For some reason, the up and down motion and going in a circle always makes me dizzy.

After the guys get off, we head over to the Sky Rockets. Okay, yeah, it goes in a circle too, but doesn't affect me like the Merry-go-Round. To get on this ride, you have to go up the ramp to the roof area over a little snack bar. It really is just a tar paper flat roof with no railing or anything. We head over to one of the "rockets," flip the little metal door open and climb in. Keith and I are in the first seat, Roger behind us. Unfortunately, Laura, a girl from our class getes in with Roger. Glad it's him and not us! A bell sounds and the ride starts. At first it moves slowly but as it picks up speed, the rockets swing out past the platform and over the people below. After a few minutes, the ride starts to slow and we gently move back over the roof as the rockets stop. Off we jump, on to the next ride—The Comet.

The Comet is my all-time favorite, and the best roller coaster ever. Even years later and dozens of other roller coaster rides, it still ranks as the best. It's not really the highest or longest. I think what is cool about it is the way it's built into the creek gorge. Right from the start, you drop straight down the hillside heading for the creek below. Then zip back up and down on some smaller hills, a hard jerk to the left as you roll past the swimming pool, then down again towards the water, only to jerk right and slow down to almost a stop at the bottom of the last hill. Then, with a hard jerk back, the front car catches on the chain drive that pulls the cars up to the top of the last hill. Here, too, you get a great view of the waterfalls that kind-of adds to the excitement. As the front car turns round the bend at the top, it seems to hang suspended, looking down the track. Suddenly it lets go and the coaster accelerates to the bottom, only to jerk back up the other side to return to the station where we unload. All I want to do is run around and get back in line. But the guys want to head to the Skooter cars next to the Comet.

We run across the strange rubbery floor of the ride to drive our own car. I go for a red one, thinking it should be faster. The other guys go for blue and green. Before the operator turns the power on, he shouts, "Remember, the less to bump, the more you ride." What? Is he kidding? This is all about bumping and hitting as many cars as you can. Power comes on and the cars start to move. Sparks flash overhead and the air fills with the smell of ozone. It truly takes skill to learn how to push the round petal to get your car to move and spin the steering wheel around to make quick turns to hit your buddy before he can hit you! After four minutes of bumping, banging and spinning, the power shuts off and the ride ends.

Next, I'm planning to head over to the train. My buddies decide it's too lame and go into the arcade to play ski ball. I'm tempted, but I love trains, and even though this is a little scaled down one, it still gives you that *click-clack* rhythm. As I enter the "station" platform, there is my aunt with my younger cousin. "Oh, good, Debbie, now you have your cousin Dave to ride with." Ahhh, really, I have to sit beside a little girl. Glad my buddies are not around.

The train blows its whistle, and the cars start to move. My cousin squeals with excitement and starts to laugh and wave at her mom. We pull out of the station over the bridge that spans Big Run, just above the waterfalls. The train runs parallel with the gravel road that goes down to the swimming area. About halfway there is a little cement tunnel covered with dirt and grass. My cousin holds her arms over her head and starts to laugh again. What is she thinking? This isn't the roller coaster. We make it to the turnaround loop and head back the same tracks to the beginning.

I team up with my buddies again and we hit the roller coaster, rockets, bumper cars, and tumble bug a couple more times. By 3:00, I'm out of money and tickets and it's time to head back to the picnic area. I split from my friends and see my mother and aunt packing up our stuff. As soon as I reach the table, I look for something left out I can eat. My mother hands me a box and says, "Come on, it's getting late and your Dad will be getting home from work soon." We head up the hill to the parking lot and load up the trunk. I get in the back seat and wave to my cousins as mom puts the Chevy in first and heads for the park exit.

On the drive home, I look back at the park to see all the kids still running from ride to ride. But I am tired and sit back with my head resting next to the window, wind blowing my stubby hair. Then I think, *the last day of school is over.*

A flash of panic hits me, "Oh no! That means there's only 87 days until school starts again!!"

Just Like Downtown

Jere Moon

During a dental appointment, Dr Watters, of Refresh Dental, reminded me of a saying that was popular during the 1950s, 'Just Like Downtown.' It meant something had gone well according to plan. Success.

In 1954, Jimmy Work wrote a country song entitled, "Just Like Downtown." Google it and listen on YouTube and the lyrics will give you an idea of what I am talking about.

During the fifties, New Castle was booming. The main street was lined with retail shops, restaurants, bakeries, theaters, florists, and many other businesses. All the stores had nicely decorated show windows. There were no empty buildings. The streets and sidewalks were swept every day. It really was something to sing about. To us, it was a mini-version of New York City. We were proud of our little town and happy to visit, or live there.

I grew up on the outskirts of New Castle. Every Friday, my mother, grandmother, younger sister Debbie, and I, went to town. We dressed up in neatly pressed dresses. My grandmother even wore a hat.

When my father and his sister, Thelma Withers, were kids, my Grandpa Moon often dropped them and my grandmother off downtown on Mercer Street on his way to work at the Greer Tin Mill. They stayed all evening until grandfather picked them up late at night on his way home. They'd watch movies at Penn, Victor, and Regent Theaters. For supper, they'd buy a pound of chipped-chopped ham and a loaf of bread at Isaly's and make sandwiches.

In between activities, they'd freshen up at the Comfort Station, a stand-alone public pay restroom that stood near the Neshannock Creek where the Rescue Mission's courtyard is today.

The women's side was maintained by a female attendant in uniform. She reminded me of an airline stewardess, except she worked for tips and collected them in a wicker bread basket. Sometimes she even put the dime in the slot of the pay stall and held the door open. After folks washed their hands at the washbowls, the attendant handed them a freshly rolled, white terry towel to dry with. On their way out, they dropped it into a hamper marked, 'soiled linens.'

A chair or two sat on each side of the sinks. Clothing was heavier then and women often became overheated and needed to sit a spell. The attendant would retreat to her supply room and return with a glass of refreshing water for them to sip on. Tips were given accordingly.

That's why, I suppose, my family had little interaction with the attendant. She usually disappeared into her supply room whenever we entered. Mom barely had a dime to get us in, let alone a tip, and if the non-pay stall was in working order, we used it.

Before we went shopping, we always stopped at a few businesses to pay bills. Mom paid with cash. We walked to Penn Power, and then hiked on to Bell Telephone. Back then, my family had a sturdy, black phone with a base that had a finger wheel for rotary dialing and an attached hand set that was held to ear and mouth with a short, curly cord connecting the two. In other words, it wasn't portable like today's phones.

We were on a party line, so conversations were seldom private. Our next-door neighbor could pick up and listen without making a sound. Sometimes we'd hear an extra click after the person we were talking to hung up and knew we'd be the topic for gossip the next day.

If Mom had money left for shopping, we journeyed up the street to G.C. Murphy's. It always smelled so good in there. The aroma of fresh-buttered popcorn permeated the air. They had a snack-bar with a long counter, stools, and booths. Mom usually gave me a dime to buy a fountain coke for my sister and I to split while she hurried off to the back of the store to pay on our lay-away.

We had rules. "Mind your manners. Don't move from your seat, talk to anyone, or take candy or anything from a stranger."

One day at Murphy's snack-bar while we were sipping our coke through two straws, I read the menu board on the wall to my sister. We agreed that someday, when we had money, we would buy one of those juicy rotisserie hot dogs that revolved in the glass case on the counter.

Nearby, a customer eating lunch, overheard and said to the waitress, "Fix those girls each a hot dog on me."

The waitress asked what we wanted on them.

"Ketchup, mustard, and relish, please." We didn't really expect her to bring them, after all, we were playing 'make believe.'

How surprised we were when she set down two real hot dogs in their white, oblong, scalloped-edged paper holders. Two! We didn't even have to share.

Fragrant steam tickled my nostrils, but I pushed them away. "We aren't allowed to take food from strangers," I said in an authoritative tone. Debbie's lower lip quivered. But hey, I was the big sister and mom depended on me to keep her safe.

"You're not taking anything from a stranger," the waitress said, pushing the hot dogs back toward us. "You're allowed to take food from a waitress." She pointed to the man in the topcoat and hat. "He's just paying the bill."

It made perfect sense to me. Besides, we'd probably be done by the time Mom returned. We grabbed those hot dogs and bit in. Juice ran down our chins.

I finished my last bite, but little sis still had the evidence in her hands, when Mom appeared.

She threw me the look. "Where did you get those?"

I glanced helplessly at the waitress as she wiped the counter beside me. I was relieved when she explained.

"A customer, who eats here every day, treated the girls."

Mom looked skeptical, but said, "That was nice of him."

From then on, Mom always made us go with her to lay-away. I hated waiting in line, even though it was usually for school clothes.

One item I'll never forget, was my package of Days of the Week underwear. They were a hot item in the fifties. The brief-style panties came in six pastel colors with Monday through Saturday written on the side along with a small design such as a ballerina, or a little girl with a duck, or a dog. There wasn't a pair for Sunday. I asked Mom why.

"The day of rest," she said.

For underwear? Do I go without? Double up on a dirty pair? I won't tell you which I did, and I didn't tell Mom either.

In the movie, *When Harry Met Sally*, Days of the Week underwear were the reason Sally's previous boyfriend, Sheldon, broke up with her. He became jealous when all of the days of Sally's underwear were accounted for except Sunday and accused her of being unfaithful.

I recall a situation that got me into a dilemma too while wearing Friday's lavender pair, my favorites by the way, beneath my new red shorts with matching pin-striped top that Mom had just gotten out of lay-away.

Every year on the last day of school, we had a picnic at Cascade Park down in the grove at one of the sheltered picnic tables, surrounded by tall hemlocks, overlooking Big Run. My Aunt Thelma and two cousins, Barb, and her younger brother, Dave, who lived in the same school district, joined us.

Aunt Thelma made her famous, fried egg sandwiches with lettuce and mayo. Mom brought brownies and lemonade. After we ate, we headed for the rides.

Even as a child, it amazed me how someone could look at a setting in and around a gorge formed by the Wisconsin Glaciation, and think, gee, this would make a great amusement park with a roller coaster that can drop off the steep sides.

The New Castle Traction Company (Later known as Penn Power) did just that. They purchased the property, then known as Big Run Falls, from Colonel Levi Brinton. Ten-year old, Edwina Norris, won ten dollars for submitting the park's new name, Cascade, during a contest. On May 29, 1897 the amusement park opened its gate.

Our park's first roller coaster was called the Toboggan, sometimes referred to as the Figure eight. In 1920, it was replaced by The Gorge, created by Billy Glenn, one of the early operators. The Comet was the park's last coaster, designed by Paul Vesco who leased and ran the park from 1952-1984.

This particular day, our mothers didn't allow us to ride the Comet. The four of us rode the mini red fire-truck that traveled through the park with its bell dinging to alert folks to clear the way. Afterwards, we climbed onto the merry-go-round with its fancy painted horses, four abreast.

Finally, my older cousin, Barb and I left our siblings at Kiddie Land with our mothers, and took off on our own adventure.

Barb and I climbed into one of the seats of the Ferris Wheel that was nestled in by a hillside. The young man who operated it, closed the bar and locked us in. The warm June breeze hit our faces as we rose. We saw Kiddie Land across the midway where our siblings were riding miniature airplanes. There was a good view of the creek that flowed through the park. Fluffy, white clouds drifted across a perfect, blue sky. It was one of those magical moments you wished would never end, joyous and carefree.

After several enjoyable spins, the operator, started letting people off, one car at a time. Even though we were the only riders left and there was a line of kids waiting to get on, Barb assured me she had powers that could give us an extra spin. She made a sign with her fingers.

It worked! We went around again.

Barb kept her fingers crossed. We cheered as we revolved a second time. Then again. And again.

We were in heaven.

Around and around we went.

After a few more rotations, I squirmed in my new underwear. My innards were beginning to feel unstable. "You can uncross your fingers anytime now, Barb. I've had enough."

But we kept circling around non-stop.

A crowd formed in the midway, their mouths agape. I spied my mother and aunt holding our sibling's hands.

Barb smiled and waved. "They can't believe we're riding so long."

I couldn't believe it either.

Meanwhile, the operator made a call on an emergency phone attached to the ride. Pay attention to us, I thought. Don't be calling someone. I want off. Now!

My stomach flipped-flopped. I took a deep breath.

Finally, an older man, in the same kind of blue uniform, broke through the crowd. He pulled hard on the ride's emergency brake.

As the wheel came to a screeching halt, our car rocked violently. We grabbed the bar with one hand and the back of the seat with our other. I was afraid I might fall out.

The crowd gasped.

Brakes whined. Inch by inch our car was lowered to the ground.

What a relief to reach the platform. The operator unlatched our bar and we ran breathlessly to our mothers to tell them all about it.

Everyone cheered. Barb thought it was for her and gave a salute with crossed fingers.

I was sure I had stained my new underwear and that they wouldn't be wearable come Sunday.

But, they were fine.

Years of underwear later, in 1982, a huge tree fell on the coaster and tracks and damaged them beyond repair. Since the other rides were getting old, that ended Cascade as an amusement park. But in 1934, Penn Power had donated the Park to the city of New Castle with one stipulation, that it be forever used for public recreation.

The City found ways to keep the park alive by capitalizing on the waterfall and rugged sylvan landscape as a lively backdrop for weddings and events. They built a playground, Bocce-ball courts, and walking trails that still attract people daily. During the Christmas season, young and old, look forward to a drive through the park to see a display of colored lights and visit with Santa.

One spring, I took the neighbor kids, Rusty and Tammy Shaffer, to the Garden Mart held at the dance hall that still remains. "We'll take a stroll through the park when we're finished buying flowers," I said.

They never had the opportunity to experience Cascade as an amusement park, so they were quite amused by my tales, especially the one about the Ferris Wheel. I showed them where it once stood.

"The Bocce-ball court is where the Tumble-bug used to be. Kiddy Land is now a playground."

We trudged back up the hill. "The city rents out the carousel building and dance hall for parties and events. What remains of the mini-train station platform makes a nice stage for outdoor bands and other activities. Pavilions in the grove are still rented out for picnics."

I mentioned the paper cones of french-fries with vinegar and salt that used to make our lips pucker. I told them about the warm, roasted peanuts we bought from Billy Glenn's red circus wagon, and pointed out the old brick chimney, all that remains of Billy's cabin built in the rocks beneath the roller coaster tracks.

As we faced the waterfalls, I showed them where the roller coaster dropped down into the gorge and crossed the creek, and then crept up the other side toward the tree tops, its wooden tracks clacking. I gestured toward the Olympic-size swimming pool and Beach House that now stand idle. "The pool used to have a crowd every day."

After we wandered into the empty picnic grove. I plopped down at my favorite table. "At the end of each school year, I picnicked here with my cousins." I pointed to the old concession stand across from the tables. "At the end of the day, we'd buy root beer snow cones there."

We continued our tour and crossed the nostalgic bridge that led to where the row boat rentals used to be. "Back then, couples paddled out to their private spot on the lake and puckered up to kiss, when their number was called over the megaphone. Boat 8. Your time is up. Please return. They'd kiss quickly and hurry back to avoid another half-hour charge. Don't ask me how I know this."

The kids giggled. "So where's the lake?"

"It used to be in this open field. In 1981, a section of the dam collapsed. When repairs proved too expensive, the water eventually drained into Big

Run." We walked the length of the field along the creek to where one section of the dam still remains.

Just then a Kingfisher sounded its high pitched "ee ee ee ee ee" as it spied a fish. A Blue Heron snatched the trout first. With wide wings flapping, the Heron flew downstream.

"Lots of things aren't here anymore," I said. "But it's still a nice place to fish, watch wildlife, and walk."

The kids eyed the birds and nodded.

Over the years, downtown New Castle, has changed too. But many things I enjoyed as a child, still remain. My dad used to take me for Coney Island Hot Dogs. I remember counting the number of buns the owner could stack up his arm while topping each wiener with meaty, hot sauce. Coney Island still draws people today, especially those who used to live here.

The New Castle Community YMCA, where I learned to swim, continues to offer lessons. The Diamond's tall fountain will be a landmark forever.

Some things weren't here before, such as Riverside Park with its mini-amphitheater for public events and concerts. We now have an open-air farmer's market where in-season produce can be purchased every Saturday. There are coffee shops that headline bands and other entertainment. Gift and specialty stores offer something for everyone. What a delight. Why, it's Just like downtown.

The River

Lavonne Lyles

As I look out on the River, I get a glimpse of life.
Everything dead goes with the flow,
No pain, no strain, no strife.
No matter where it's going, the current's endless rage,
Just ride the river of no return, to set the final stage.
Too late now, can't turn back.
The end of comfort's bliss, a life of no real meaning,
An epitaph like this.

The Street Walker

Lavonne Lyles

A slave to men's passion, a slave to men's lust.
How will it read on your grave in the dust?
As you stroll down the street and show off your ware,
Is your conscience so seared that our heart doesn't care?
Or was if for money you ransomed your soul?
Was it for money that sin takes its toll.
Oh, lonely street walker, God walks with you too.
You sadden his heart with the things that you do.
Whatever your reason for leading this life,
It brings only misery, hatred and strife.
Many a man makes their bed down in hell,
Because of the story, you don't wanna tell.

Unforgettable New Castle

Kathy Hosler

I grew up in the country about eight miles from New Castle, Pennsylvania. As a small girl in the 1950's, I seldom got to go to the big town, but, when my mother took my brothers and me, the hustle and bustle of the huge metropolis really impressed us. Cars, buses, and people were everywhere. It was nothing like our quiet life in the country.

A trip to Kirk Hutton's on Washington Street was an unforgettable experience. They had everything you could imagine. From tools to toys to household small appliances, the store was crammed with items from floor to ceiling.

I remember the time I was fascinated by a toy/musical instrument called a bell organ. It was about 18 inches wide and just as tall. A Christmas tree shaped tower of bells with a keyboard. When you pressed a key, a corresponding bell rang and you could actually play songs.

I was mesmerized. That's all I talked about for weeks, but its $30 price tag was almost half of my father's weekly paycheck, so I never got it.

When we needed school shoes, we went to Penney's. In those days, a salesman would have you stand on a foot measuring instrument (called the Brannock Device) to determine the size and width of your foot. Then he would disappear into the back room, bring out several pair of shoes, and put them on your feet. He instructed you to walk up and down the aisle to see how they felt to you. He would push on your toes and say, "you still have some growing room in these." That was always important to a mom. Then it was up to my mother to choose the pair I would get.

I always loved going to Neisners. I don't remember too much about the store except that they had a huge selection of wonderful candy. My big brother, Skip, and I were allowed to get one thing every time we went in. One of our favorites was the Foxy Loxy Doctor's Candy Pill Kit which contained several clear glass bottles about the size that spices come in now. They were filled with assorted colors of candy pills.

It came with instructions, such as, "For a stubbed toe, take 2 yellow pills," or "for a wrenched back, take 1 green pill." So my brother and I would 'accidentally' stub our toes until all the yellows were gone and then on to the next 'injury'. Do you suppose this is how some hypochondriacs got their start?

G.C. Murphy's had to be my all-time favorite store. As soon as you stepped inside, the aroma of freshly popped popcorn greeted you. It was a real treat. They also had a wonderful lunch counter that served some of the best ice cream specialties around.

Every time I went into Murphy's, I made a beeline to their pet department. They had birds that chirped and sang. It was really amazing to see them close up. And, there was a large assortment of colorful fish in big tanks. They also had colorful dyed chicks and ducks at Easter. I always thought they were born those bright colors.

Plus, their toy department had more toys than I had ever seen. Mrs. Santa Claus was at Murphy's every December. I wasn't so sure about talking to Santa when I was little, but I would eagerly tell his wife what I wanted for Christmas.

Not all of my memories of New Castle are about the stores downtown. Let me tell you about a day I spent at Cascade Park that my family will never forget....

My father worked as a machinist at the Johnson Bronze in New Castle. Their company picnic was held every summer at Cascade Park. The one we went to when I was 5 years old was just about the best day of my young life. At least it started out that way.

My father, mother, and 3 brothers - 8 year old Skip, 3 year old Jim, and my baby brother, Billy - piled into our car and headed for the Park.

The picnic grove featured huge tables loaded with every kind of food imaginable. And, they had pop to drink, as much as you wanted. We almost never got pop at our house. We ate and drank until we could hold no more.

Then it was time for games. The best and most fun one was the Money Hunt. We kids were sorted into groups according to our age, and we stood in a circle around huge piles of sawdust (at least the size of 2 large contractor wheelbarrows). Buried throughout the sawdust were more pennies, nickels, dimes, and even quarters than I had ever seen.

A whistle blew, we made a mad dash, and started digging through sawdust for the treasured coins. We got to keep everything we found. I got seventy-two cents. Wow, I thought I was rich! Could this day get any better?

Why yes, yes it could. The children of Johnson Bronze employees got to go on all the rides they wanted to for free.

My brother, Skip, and I enjoyed a ride on the train that circled the park, then tried out the Tumblebug and the Merry go Round. Next, we had a go at the Dodge-em cars. It was all so exciting and so much fun.

Then we came to the Ferris Wheel. I had never seen anything so grand. I begged Skip to take me on it, and he did. We got in the gondola seat, and the safety bar clicked shut to hold us in.

Soon, I was sailing up into the clouds. I couldn't believe it. I had never been so high. I could see far out into the distance and everyone on the ground looked so little. We went round, and round, and round. I loved it!

The Ferris Wheel stopped, and I thought our ride was over. But no, it started going again - this time backwards. Round and round we went.

Suddenly, I didn't feel so good. There were butterflies in my stomach. I told Skip that I was sick and wanted off. Each time our gondola passed the ride operator, he waved his arms wildly and screamed, "Stop! My sister is sick. Stop!"

Well you can guess what happened next. That's right. All the picnic food in my five year old tummy was now on me, my brother, and our seat. Since we were near the top of the ride, some of it also cascaded onto the kids below, and even on the ride operator.

He wasted no time unloading all the people from the ride. He was really angry and hollered at me as he let us out. My brother stuck up for me and said, "Why didn't you stop? I kept yelling for you to stop. Why didn't you stop?"

We were a mess. That was the end of the fun day at Cascade Park for us. We got in the car and headed home. Skip, and I in the back seat, and my father, mother, and baby brother, Billy, in the front. Jim demanded to sit in the front seat too. He wouldn't sit anywhere near us.

Just as we were leaving the New Castle, city limits, I stood on the seat and leaned over my dad's shoulder. "Daddy, I think I am going to be sick again!" I whispered urgently.

Unfortunately for my dad and his shirt, I was right.

Savannah Methodist Church Haunting

Susan Urbanek Linville

David Barge was born in 1840, the son of Leonard and Martha Barge. His life was filled with hard work on the family's Shenango farm. Every day he rose early to help his father and older brother Jacob milk the cows and check for eggs in the hen house before tending the fields. The only respite from the daily chores was Sunday morning services at the Savannah Methodist Church, a short walk from the farm across open fields and through shadowy woods.

When David was twenty, the presidential election was the talk of the town. Abraham Lincoln won the contest in early November, but not all the farmers were happy. There were rumors of war and, in December of that year, South Carolina seceded the Union. David was frightened and exhilarated at the same time. He had learned about the Revolutionary War and all its heroes in school. Maybe he could be a hero too.

The following year, more states left the union. In March 1861, there was news of an uprising at Fort Sumter. By July, the United States was at war with itself. David joined the 1st Light Artillery, Company B under the command of Captain Cooper, but war was not the romantic adventure that he expected. It began with long days marching and traveling east to Camp Berry in Washington, D.C. They stayed there until August 14th when they left for Maryland.

David's days were filled with marches and battles: Manassas in March, Falmouth in April, Mechanicsville in June. The Seven Days Battles, Richmond, Mechanicsville, Gaines's Mill, and Harrison's Landing followed. He witnessed the loss of life and limb. At the Second Battle of Bull Run, August 30, 1862, he was one of the injured. He was medically discharged and could have gone home, but he was bound by duty and joined the 2nd Union Volunteer Calvary for another year.

After three years in the war, David did not return home feeling like a hero. He would wake in the middle of the night in a cold sweat thinking he was camped in an open field. Loud noises brought back the terror of cannon fire. He couldn't get rid of the memories of severed limbs outside the medical tents, calls for help from men in the fields, wounds bleeding into the dirt.

David could have taken over the duties of running the family farm, but the memories of war followed him too closely. He let his younger brother, George, take charge. David worked as a general laborer and was happy to be alone with himself. His one comfort in life was attending Savannah Church. The scriptures provided solace and eased the recollections of the bitter battles he'd witnessed.

David enjoyed a daily routine of farm chores and Sunday church services until one cold Thursday evening in November 1869. It was time to light the church for its weekly prayer meeting. David left the farmhouse with lantern in hand and walked across the stubbled farm field east of the barn. A partial moon hung low in the sky, occasionally blotted out by a stray cloud. He held his coat tight to keep out the wind.

Leaves crunched underfoot as he entered a copse of sycamores and elms. Wood smoke from surrounding farms soured the cold night air. He followed a narrow footpath worn into the ground by his family's Sunday trips to the church. Wind froze his cheeks and he wondered if anyone would come out on such a blustery night.

The single story, wood framed church, built just 15 years before, nestled against the woods. Two entrance doors faced the rutted country road, and a modest fence surrounded the church and its small graveyard. David entered the holy grounds through the gate and stood outside awaiting the parishioner's arrival. No one came.

David checked the doors to make sure they were secure against the wind. He hadn't taken more than a few steps when the thing appeared before him. Hair raised across David's arms and neck. It was human shaped, but not a man. He had seen his share of bears wandering in the woods and this was no bear. It was white, coalesced out of the moonlight into a ghostly figure. A spirit? His heart raced. A demon?

David ran. He leaped the fence and raced to the woods. He fled wildly between the trees. Gun shots echoed in his memory. When he reached the field, his feet pounded over the hard soil. Vivid memories of cannon fire exploded all around him. Don't look back, he told himself. He gasped for breath, breathing in frigid air. Don't stop.

Warm yellow light flickered in the Barge farmhouse windows ahead. Almost home, he reassured himself. He didn't slow until he rounded the barn. When he burst into the kitchen, his sister-in-law looked up from the sink filled with soapy water. His brother, George, and two grown nephews, Eli and John, sat at the table.

"What's the matter," Jennette asked

David caught his breath. "Nothing," he said. "No one showed up at the church."

"You're as white as a sheet," she said.

"I'm fine." He retreated to the living room and stood near the fire, holding his hands out to warm them.

George followed him into the room and sat in an old wooden rocker that belonged to their mother. "What has happened, David?"

"I don't want to talk about it."

Eli and John joined them "It looks like you've seen a ghost, Uncle David," Eli said. "What put the scare into you?"

"Something not of this world," David said. After his hands warmed, he sat and told them what he had witnessed.

The next evening, Eli and John visited their friend, Leander, on whose father's land the church had been built. Eli invited him outside and they told him the story of what Uncle David had seen.

"He's pulling your leg," Leander said.

"If you saw the look on his face you would know it was no joke," Eli said. "Uncle David is not a storyteller."

Leander kicked the frozen ground with his boot. "There's no such things as ghosts."

"That's what I think too." John pointed across the field. "We are going to go see for ourselves."

"It's almost dark." Leander said.

Eli gazed across the field. He wanted to believe there were no ghosts, but Uncle David wasn't a liar. He wouldn't have made up the story. Eli thought of himself as brave, but he wasn't sure he wanted to witness this wayward spirit. "Are you afraid?" he asked Leander.

"No," Leander said. "Let's go."

The night was cold, and their breath floated into the darkness as they crossed the rutted rows of the field. The moon peeked from beneath a cloud, casing long shadows as they crossed the woods. When they reached the church, Eli pulled his coat close and tucked his hands in his pockets. Maybe Uncle David had scared the spirit away and they'd see nothing.

They waited silently in the darkness on the front steps of the building, scanning the surrounding fields and graveyard. The scent of dead leaves drifted around them.

"No ghost is coming," Leander said. "Just as I said."

John laughed nervously.

"Maybe Uncle David was having a war memory," Eli said. "Sometime things come back to him."

"Well, I'm going home," Leander said. "It's too cold to be standing around here."

A white form moved around the corner of the church.

"There," John said.

The eerie figure looked like a man in a coat with legs that didn't quite reach the ground. Instead of walking like a normal man, it glided toward them like it was on wheels.

Hair rose on Eli's neck and arms. His cheeks warmed.

"What is it?" Leander cowered behind John.

"I'm not staying to find out." Eli took off across the cemetery. Leander and John sprinted after him. They didn't stop until they reached Leander's farmhouse. Eli bent over to catch his breath. John looked back across the field.

"Do you think it will follow us?"

Eli hadn't thought about that possibility. "I think we'll be getting home now," he said.

Eli and John hurried across the field to their own house. When they entered the kitchen, Uncle David was sitting at the table smoking his pipe and reading the evening newspaper.

"You boys are out late," David said.

Eli shrugged. They didn't say another word about the thing the rest of the evening.

The next night, John convinced Eli to return to the church. This time, they invited a fourth friend, Isaac, who lived nearby. Safety in numbers, they thought. Maybe it wouldn't be so scary this time. They met in the barn behind Leander's house. The cows inside huffed and pawed at the straw, expecting to be fed again. Instead, Leander removed a lantern from a peg by the door.

"I think you are all daft," Isaac said. "It's probably someone in a sheet playing a prank."

Leander lit a lantern. "It made a believer of me."

"We all witnessed it," Eli said.

They walked single file from the barn and across the field.

"And you're sure it was a ghost?"

"It was something not of this earth," John said. "White. Like a cloud."

They entered the woods. Lantern light flickered off the trees, casting wavering shadows. When they reached the front steps of the small church, Eli covered the lantern. They stood in darkness for what seemed like an hour. Please don't return, he prayed. Maybe the spirit had found its way back to its own realm.

"I don't see anything," Isaac said.

"Just wait. It..."

"There," John said. A white form appeared in the graveyard. It made no sound as it crossed the frost covered grass and crunchy leaves.

"Oh my God," Isaac whispered.

"Stand your ground," John said.

The specter drew closer and closer. Eli forced himself to remain still despite the screaming urge to run. His heart thudded. His hands grew damp.

"What is it?" Isaac asked.

The figure stopped a few strides from them, its form undulating like smoke, and then it drifted away toward the rear of the church. It stopped by a small tree. Scratching sounds filled the quiet, like a cat sharpening its claws on the bark. Eli shivered.

"It must be one of Satan's minions," Leander whispered.

It vanished from its spot near the tree and reappeared near the cemetery. When it evaporated a second time and reemerged near them, Eli let out a gasp.

"What do you want?" Leander yelled.

It groaned as if trying to speak and vanished again.

The next time they saw the thing, it glided across the graveyard and through the fence.

"Let's go after it," John said. Leander and Isaac followed. Eli brought up the rear. This was a bad idea. What if it led them straight to hell?

They reached the fence and climbed over. The thing paused at the end of the woods, but as they drew near, it retreated.

Eli's teeth chattered. "I think we should stop this."

"Why?" John asked. "Are you afraid?"

"He's right," Leander said. "We need to bring others to help us."

Forty-eight years later, witnesses spoke to David P. Jackson of the New Castle News about the haunting of Savannah Methodist Church. The newspaper account ends with the following:

"The boys now thought they were justified in making the matter public and the news spread like wildfire among the farmers, causing great excitement for miles around. The next evening a large crowd gathered at the church with firearms and implements but no ghost appeared. Perhaps it did not like crowds or perhaps the runaway spirit from Tarturus had been recaptured by the keepers and taken back to its gloomy prison. At any rate it was never seen again. The crowd searched the graveyard, and the church from basement to garret, but nothing was found to throw any light on the mystery nor has anything been discovered since to explain it."

David P. Jackson, "The Ghost at Savannah Church," New Castle News, February 26, 1917.

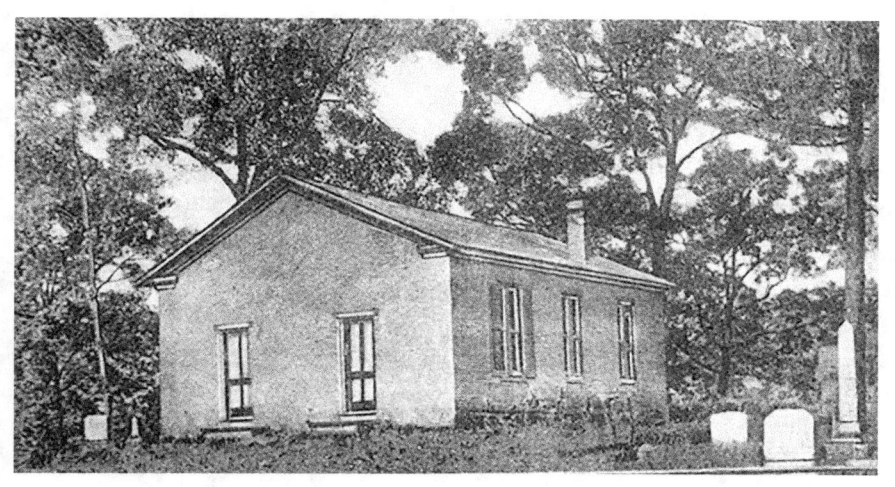

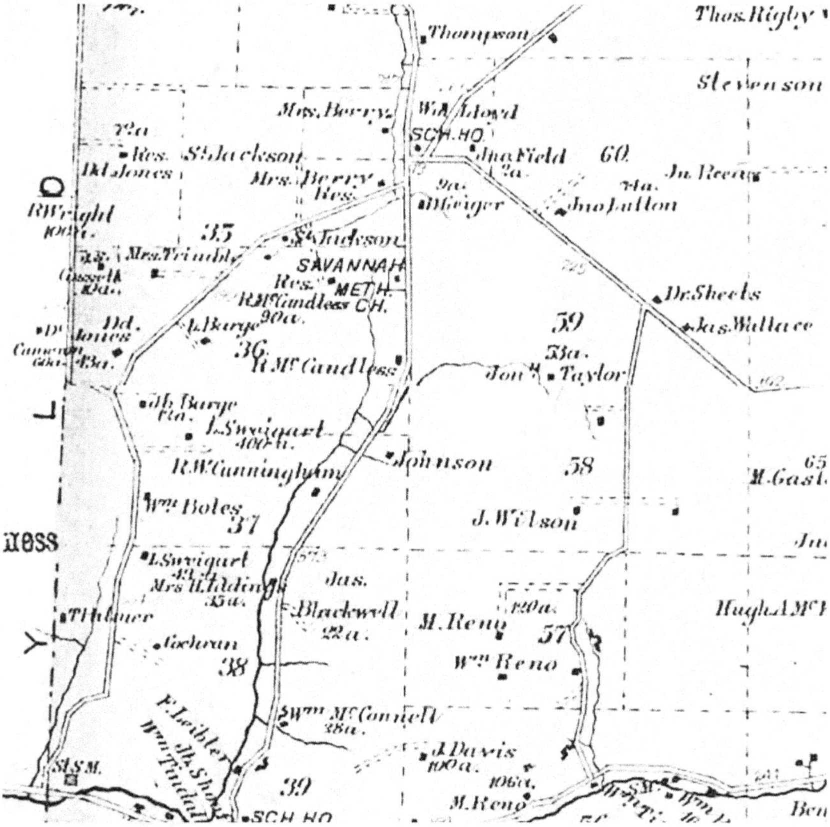

Thos. Rigby
Thompson
Stevenson
Mrs. Berry
SCH. HO.
St. Jackson
Jno. Field
60
Dd. Jones
Mrs. Berry Res.
Jno. Fulton
R. Wright
35
Mrs. Trimble
SAVANNAH
METH. CH.
Dr. Sheets
Jas. Wallace
59
36
R. McCandless
Taylor
L. Swigart
400a.
Johnson
R.W. Cunningham
58
Wm. Boles
37
J. Wilson
L. Swigart
Jas. Blackwell
22a.
M. Reno
57
Wm. Reno
38
Cochran
Wm. McConnell
28a.
J. Davis
100a.
39
M. Reno
SCH. HO.

Nowadays

Richard G. Yates, Jr.

1 Gideons

"I will be at the business meeting tomorrow at 6 pm then leave can't afford to eat."

"If you want to stay (I would like to see you there), we will take care of dinner. We understand your situation, but don't let that you keep you from staying. I just write a check from the camp fund for all the dinners, so don't worry about it. So, plan to stay for dinner and meeting ok?"

"Please understand I would like whatever money I give to go towards the pastors' appreciation breakfast. I really don't want to have anything there."

"You don't need to give anything to have dinner – it's ok."

"I'm having a hard time with this. I may not come at all tomorrow."

"You should not think that way – you do a lot to help the camp, and everyone likes and respects you. No reason not to come!"

"I'll probably go. It's like home to me even though I'm a charity case."

"You are a valued brother in Christ that's what you are! You come and enjoy dinner, the meeting, and the fellowship with your Gideon family. See you there!"

"Thank you."

"I will be attending tonight and will eat, but I don't think I'll be able to stay the whole meeting. I work early tomorrow and got to get rest if possible. I hope you understand."

"That's fine; see you there."

2 But the economy is booming!!

3 Upward Mobile – Reward for 17 years of faithfulness

4 Prelude to Prayer Breakfast

Before the breakfast at Tanner's, the guys typically talk about hunting for deer, turkeys, coyotes, etc. We see various pictures of animals shot or still alive on trail cameras. In fishing season, there are pictures of fish caught in various places.

Last week, I read an article about cash assistance ending in PA.

5 Getting Ready

I vividly remember Mom getting ready for church by the sound of high heeled shoes click clicking quickly. Many times I was late getting ready. But the memory of the click clicking lives on – it's a poignant remembrance of the way life was.

6 James Montgomery 08/04/2019

James is 91; he is fine with me using his name in this piece. I met James early on in my stay here in New Castle. At first, I was still at the City Rescue Mission. Later I had gone to live in Mom's house.

He has worked at Precision Feed Screws as a janitor since I've known him. He is like a father to me.

My volunteer tutoring classes were at his house on Neal Street for the most part. We worked on reading and a little math. His big accomplishment was studying for and passing the driver's test for his driver's license.

We went fishing, and I went to activities like plays that his granddaughter was in.

Just last week we met up at Burger King again for a Slushie (his treat) and seeing his granddaughter and great grandchildren.

What a wonderful friend!

7 Ferrari

I came to where I work to buy a cell phone cord.

"The car is old; the cigarette lighter connection may not be very good. The situation is precarious."

"Time to get a new car – Ferrari!"

"The car has to last forever."

(See preceding: "Upwardly Mobile.")

8 Yet Another Friend

This friend I have known for a long time. We were in the Lords of the Castle Barbershop Chorus together – both baritones.

He was in various good quartets.

He has a very kind giving heart.

9 Sam

Sam has been a friend for a long time.

He towed for the previous owner of the gas station where I work. When the station was sold, he got another towing job but was hurt in an accident and had to retire.

He has had a lot of experience in towing.

He is very friendly and always makes my day to see him!

10 Pilot Stop

I stop by Pilot on 422 on the way to most anywhere – my girlfriend's, Butler VA, or longer trips East.

It is a good place to relax with my 91 cent senior coffee and a book.

11 "When Doves Cry" Memories

"When Doves Cry" by Prince still plays in many places – like Wendy's Neshannock or even that Pilot stop.

When it plays it always reminds me of that love crush of long ago at "Shawn's" when I fell madly in love with "Lisa." I was a cook; she was a beautiful sexy waitress with fiery eyes.

12 Struggling

Her sign said: "Struggling need help with food gas." With her was her daughter under an umbrella to keep out the sun and a little puppy on a leash.

I gave her $2; I said I was struggling too. She said the cost of living was too high for everybody.

I said, "Many people are doing well, but many people aren't. It's like a great divide."

She said, "Never give up."

I said, "That's what we got to do."

I walked back to my car at Pilot and drove off.

13 Mileage Pay

I wasn't able to get mileage pay at the VA today for the 54 mile round trip. I do not have a combat injury. My income would have to be $14,000 to get it. With everything I do probably get $30,000 a year. But: I am extremely grateful for the free care I get at the VA thanks to low income.

14 Encouragement

I was entering the gym; I had the preconceived notion that I wasn't feeling the energy or motivation to do much on the treadmill – maybe 5 minutes.

Then I entered. An old friend using the bicycle said, "You're late." It was happenstance.

I said, "You've motivated me to do more just seeing you."

So I did 15 minutes on the treadmill.

15 The Unexpected

At Wendy's, my coffee experience is an adventure. If you see me, you can ask me about it.

One thing I can report on here is that many times at one Wendy's in town I receive a coffee for eleven cents off – like a senior discount - 94 cents.

But I went to the other Wendy's. I had my dollar ready but not the 5 cents for the regular priced $1.05 coffee. So, when the clerk asked for $1.05 my absent minded self was frustrated – the unexpected happened – I was at the other Wendy's. What should I expect?

16 Prejudice

I was hired in 2002. When the gas station was sold in 2015, I had seen many employees come and go. All these employees were of one race – guess?

17 Wendy's Lunch

Another nice crowd at Wendy's. It's like home to me.

18 Stock Market Dip 08-14-2019

The stock market dipped 3% today.

My boss said, "Time to buy."

I said, "Sure; I'll sink 1 billion in it."

Certainly I can do that with my $793 a month Social Security and $8 an hour plus tips pumping gas, etc.

19 At My Wit's End

I get glimpses of the Lord when I'm at my wit's end and when nothing else works. It should be all the time.

20 Bottom of the Barrel Revisited 08-16-2019

I had been eating at a local family restaurant and told the waitress of 30 plus years about my book "A Love Book" about going from teaching in Brazil to minimum wage cooking in PA.

She had said I went to the bottom of the barrel.

Then on March 17, 2019 the restaurant closed. My friend has said that that building will be empty ten years from now.

21 Another Revisited

All the employees under my new employer at the gas station have been one race – guess?

22 Preview of Gideon Work 08-16-2019

Tonight I, poverty stricken, work with two people – of upstanding successful people. I feel out of place already. We are to give the Word of God – New Testaments and Bible App Cards – to passers-by at the Fair. Maybe I'll just leave early.

I stayed an hour. I felt God wanted me to be there.

23 10 Cents

"It's 10 cents more if you pump it?"

A nod.

"That's bull shit."

24 Count Your Blessings

My friend saw a disabled girl at the store.

This made him say, "Count your blessings."

25 Gas Station, Tuesday, August, 27, 2019 3-9 Shift

I arrived early to seeing that the pumps were closed due to a line test. I told my man employer of the couple that I'd come back in at 4 pm, as the pumps would be down for an hour.

I returned before 4 to a full parking lot, so I parked by the U Hauls.

I started my shift pumping gas and parking my bag of books and lunch pail by the bench outside. I would soon be sitting there.

The first 20 minutes were busy; cars one after another came to be pumped. I amassed about $8 in tips. Then it slowed down.

I was reading "The Evangelicals" by Frances Fitzgerald. I had received my direct deposit stub for the previous two weeks: about $328 take home for 48 hours of work. I was busy finding my check register out of one of the bags.

"Richard, it's slow. Can you roll blue bags? You can finish your food."

I left my little bag open on the bench and went inside. Two 10 packs of blue bags were on the pumper's chair for me to roll. I'm bad at rolling blue bags. Maybe with practice I can get better.

"I'm getting a headache."

"Oh, no."

I roll the bags badly.

I pump a few cars.

"Richard, I need you to roll these bags over."

"No. One time is enough. I won't waste time rolling them again."

"Keep your voice down."

"I will talk loudly!"

"Richard, you will not read anymore."

"Yes, I will read!"

I was thinking of just walking out, but out on the bench I talked on the phone to my girlfriend, sister and brother-in-law, and brother. I calmed down.

I performed my duties of pumping gas and turning in money without talking to my employer. Time went by. In down times I continued reading my book.

Time came to clean up the coffee area, sweep and mop, and take out trash.

"I see the car! You don't have to tell me." I pumped a car.

I went back outside on the bench after I had cleaned up and read and pumped a few cars.

I came in and shut off the cooler lights at 8:45 pm. I called my sister and told her I could be fired, and, if I was fired, I would say ok and not beg for my job back as I had long ago with restaurant jobs.

The owner lady returned, probably with supper for both of them.

At 8:55 pm, I turned off the "open" light and politely asked for the locks to lock the pumps.

I waited and pumped one last car before locking the pumps.

I turned in the money silently, said nothing, opened the store door and locked it.

The owner man unlocked the door and came out.

"Here is your final pay."

"OK."

"Thank you."

And life goes on.

Rapid Tappits Still Up and Running

Dorothy Knight Burchett

Who would have thought that a few teenagers gathering together on the running boards of their cars in 1955 would form an organization that is still alive in 2020?

Jack Stewart and Dale Fruehstorfer are the two remaining members of the Rapid Tappits, an antique car club in New Castle, that now has 60 members. They got their name from the flathead Ford engines in the cars many of the 14 original members had. According to Stewart, the engines made a loud tapping sound when it was running and seemed to lend well as a name for the group.

Although the group started in 1955, there was a long break, as teenage boys became husbands and fathers, but restarted in 1988 with 20 members.

Stewart's car, when he was 17 years old, was a 1947 Plymouth 2-door sedan. It was a jalopy, and instead of paint, sported a fine coat of primers, as Stewart says he could not afford to paint it.

Some of the other cars owned by the young men were a 1927 Willys Knight and a couple of Hupmobiles. Stewart mentions a time when the adventurous and mischievous boys "butted into a parade in a Hupmobile. The announcers didn't know what to announce. The band was far behind, because the Hupmobile made so much smoke."

The group's favorite pastime, prior to their marriages, was hanging out at Smith's Dairy on Old Rte. 422 in Shenango or Zingaro's Dairy at the corner of Ellwood and Princeton Roads.

There, they played the pinball machines and talked about "cars and girls," says Stewart. One of their escapades consisted of the boys pulling up close to the telephone booth at Zingaro's, calling the state police and revving up their loud mufflers. They hurriedly backed up their cars, parked, ran into the dairy store and began playing the pinball machines. They had barely got started when the police came through the door and said, "You boys having a little fun?"

"They knew just where to come," says Stewart.

The young jalopy owners also liked to drag race and spent many a Sunday afternoon at the 1/4-mile drag strip at Howland Corners, near Youngstown OH. "There was one guy, I don't remember his name," says Stewart. "I just couldn't beat him. He had a '55 Chevy and so did I."

Stewart says the drag race nearly cost him his marriage. "This one fellow called me," he relates, "and asked me if I wanted to drag race and I said sure. The only thing is, I was supposed to be getting married soon and I was supposed to go to her parents' house to get some furniture and move it to the apartment we had rented. Her mother said if my wife-to-be couldn't depend on me to be there then, what kind of husband would I be."

They did get married, though, and his wife, Nancy, has accompanied him in his adventures as a Rapid Tappit, along with the wives of many of the other members.

Some of those adventures of the group include the James Dean Run in Fremont IN; trips to Gettysburg and Altoona. They sponsored the soap box derby in New Castle in 1996 and 1997; as well as The Great Race in 1996. They provided a luncheon for the cross-country racers and the History Channel broadcast the event. A memorable event for the men and their wives was the time the group rented a bus in the early 1990s and spent the weekend in Niagara Falls.

At this time in their lives, the boys have grown into men, but their interest in old cars has not faded. Some of them own more than one antique car and are proud to show them off. They and their wives go to car shows and cruise-ins when the weather allows. Their main event is to go to the Hugger Mugger parking lot on the East Side, on Wednesday evenings, where disk jockey Greg Marshall, from Union, spins records from the '50s and '60s. They also participate in the Dustoff, a car cruise-in, at Shenango High School in May. They have had 26 of them, according to Dale Fruehstorfer.

Fruehstorfer recalls that Dan's Garage, at the corner of Rtes. 422 and 388, was a place where the group used to hold meetings and work on their cars. He says he misses the old times when the men and their wives used to sit outside and listen to '50s and '60s music until 11:00 at night. He adds that the membership fees and money gathered from the annual Dustoff, mostly go to local charities, such as the Salvation Army and the Rescue Mission.

Says Fruehstorfer, "I just hope we can get back together again. Everybody in the group is real friendly. We had as many as 100 members at one time"

Now you will see the group in their lawn chairs under their canopies to shelter them from the hot sun at various car shows and cruise-ins. They don't talk about girls anymore, but they still talk about cars.

Denise Yoho Guthery

The old First Federal Building (originally). Since the mid 1950s it has been a unique building in downtown New Castle, and it just doesn't seem that it was that long ago it was full of doctors, stores, sounds of carillon bells, and a large beautiful bank. Soon its future will soon be another parking lot and it will be just another memory of what was in downtown New Castle.

The Golden Bowl

Joseph Kearney

The morning clouds awaken
From dark passage
Over dark blue fields
The sun rising in the east
Calls the spirits from the air
They cry without ceasing
Mercy Mercy Mercy
On the trees and the corn
Green in the fields of life

Sins of Cinema

Randy Ryan

Very few people knew that, along a main stretch in downtown New Castle, Pennsylvania, there lay the birthplace of Warner Brothers' cinematic movie theater. At least it seemed that way to Edward Johns. Various children, and even teenagers and people who fell into the category of young adults, when he would try to pick their brains to garner information—or at least quotes—for the book he was writing, were completely ignorant to this. Amazing, but somehow not surprising, especially when considering digital times. He walked along the sidewalk in front of the River Plex, the building in which the theater was located. The River Plex was striking, complete with pillars, balconies, American flags, and escalators on the other side of the glass doors, but the real magic, Edward knew, lay within.

"Can I help you, sir?"

The voice snapped Edward out of his stupor. He turned and saw a man who was dressed like a meter maid standing along the curb. In his hand he held a pen and pad, probably writing tickets.

"Uh, yes," Edward said. He walked towards the meter maid man and extended his hand. "My name is Edward Johns. I called and spoke to someone on the city council recently. I believe her name was Alice. I had an appointment to come and look at the entrance of the theater from one to two."

The meter maid man took Edward's hand and shook it delicately. It was about as limp a dead-fish handshake that you could ask for. Edward quickly pulled his hand back.

"You see it's for a book I'm writing," Edward continued. "They told me I could go inside, have a look around, and take a few photographs. The book itself will be part of the New Castle History series. Like I said, I'll mostly be scoping out the entrance. I know that the doors that lead into the theater are locked."

"I see," the meter maid man said.

"Well, do you think you could let me in?" Edward said.

"That shouldn't be a problem," the meter man said. He unhooked a keychain full of silver and brass keys from his beltloop and thumbed through them until he found the right one. "Normally, they wouldn't give someone in my position a key to the building, but in my case, they were willing to make an exception. I guess it doesn't have so much to do with me, but with the fact that you have a scheduled visit. That's all I need to know, really."

"What exactly is it that you do?" Edward asked.

"Well, I'm in charge of a lot of things," the meter man said. "Name's Tim, by the way. Parking, maintenance, watering all the ferns you see hanging from the lampposts up and down the streets. I'm a jack of all trades, really, corny as that may sound."

Edward turned and took one last look at the sunlit world of downtown New Castle as Tim unlocked the door. *Time to enter the place not as brightly lit, like that Tales from The Darkside show.*

"It would be easy to get lost in here," Tim said as they walked inside. "Especially if you had no idea what you were looking for. This place is like a museum. I guess that makes me the curator."

Edward pulled out his trusty iPhone and waved it. "This is my camera in case you're wondering. So much better than lugging around those old, clunky things."

"I hear you," Tim said as he and Edward walked through the entryway. "You know, it's the invention of things like that, partly, that are the reason that beautiful places like this are largely forgotten."

"You know I was just thinking that when I arrived," Edward said.

"Once we get up to the second floor," Tim said, "you will see the entrance straight ahead. You won't need a tour guide for that." He laughed at his own joke. "Take as long as you need to. I'll be the first to tell you, there's not really much to see. The door that leads into the actual theater is always locked." They reached the second-floor balcony. The double doors with the sign reading WARNER BROTHERS was, indeed, directly ahead. "I'll be outside. Come and find me when you are ready to leave. Believe me, I'm becoming more and more forgetful. The chances are high that I would lock you in here overnight. I know you didn't make an appointment for a slumber party."

Edward chuckled. "Thanks a lot, Tim. I really appreciate it."

Tim smiled, nodded, and was on his way back down the spiral staircase He was right. There really wasn't all that much to this place. Then again, all he had access to was the entrance. He walked up to the doors. He stopped to snap a photo here and there as he got closer. The doors were closed, locked, a literal and physical barrier between the past and present. He let out a sigh, reached and grabbed the doorknob, and twisted and turned. He knew that he would be met with the sudden halt of locked blots—but he was not—because the doorknob turned, the inner gears released, and the door opened. He gasped, in utter surprise. *They must have forgotten to lock the doors. But how?* Truthfully, it did not matter. He could sneak inside.

Without another thought, he slipped in. The hallway was carpeted, but the carpeting was old, faded, and torn, and the walls and ceiling, he could see thanks to his flashlight, had exposed patches of pink insulation covered by plastic, as well as what looked like splotches of freshly applied plaster.

Lining the hallway were doors, judiciously spaced apart, that lead into each individual theatre. He had learned throughout the course of his research that they had added a big screen to the small theater, but he was oddly unaware of the further renovations that made everything see so old.

He walked into the nearest theater. His iPhone light beamed a path as he entered the door. Something was off. The seats were old-fashioned, not the high-backed, sturdy chairs he knew had long replaced them, and the screen was a sheet, as opposed to the smartboard-like contraption that showed film and video in high definition.

He walked down the declining isle alongside the few rows of seats and came to the base of the silver screen. It was not tall, even while standing at the foot of it. He reached out and touched it. It felt cold and smooth against his fingers, and rippled like the waves of the ocean, or one of those aluminum, metallic-colored pieces of plastic that sounded like thunder when you shook it. His light was not trained on the screen. After all, it was blank. He stopped pressing against it, and his fingers slid slowly down its length. He slowly turned.

The darkness of the theater seemed misty, almost cloudy or foggy. It had an unmistakable smell, cigarette smoke. Maybe it was a trick of the light or his clouded field of vision, but he could have sworn that, at the right angel, he could see shadowy figures sitting in the seats. Near the ceiling, a small square of light cut through the smokiness. At the center of this small, lighted square was something that looked clear and circular. It made the tell-tale clicking sound that he remembered well.

The projectionist booth. Getting good, clear pictures of that would be worth more, or perhaps just cooler, than dark photos of an empty old theatre. Edward walked back up the aisle. Thankfully, there was a doorway behind the last rows of seats that lead straight up to it. He reached out to test it. Open. Thank the stars.

The flight of steps leading to the top was rather small, and narrow. Dim, yellow light illuminated the stairway and the room at the pinnacle. He switched the light on his phone off. He needed to save the battery as it was. He slid it back into his pocket.

When he reached the top, his breath was stolen away. The room was small, almost two by four, but old newspaper clippings, old movie tickets, and even things like fliers, brochures, and pamphlets, were taped and tacked to the walls, and scattered about the old floor. He could tell this hadn't been used in a long time (naturally) but whoever used to work it must not have been very tidy. He thought he recognized some of the papers, recognized them from childhood. *This couldn't have been where dad worked. He worked at Westgate, not this one.*

For some reason, he couldn't remember. The truth was, he didn't care to remember, at least not when he noticed the old, black reel of film, complete with the big, old-fashioned loop and all, peeking its long, round neck out of the square hole in the front of the office. Mesmerized, he walked towards it, and his felt his knees go weak, threatening to buckle, when he realized that there was still film, *fresh* film, black and shiny, reeled through the machine, seemingly ready to project.

Something told him that he was going to get it to work. Maybe it was hasty thinking, maybe it was instinct. Then again, maybe it would not have anything to show him at all.

It had been so long, he hardly remembered how to work one of these things. If he remembered correctly, it was not much different than operating a camera. He remembered all those times going to work with his dad—at Westgate, right—and his dad showing him the craft of his trade, feeding the film through the circle, and projecting beautiful images upon the screen through the bluish lighting. Oddly, everything seemed prepared and ready to go. Even more strange, the projector seemed modern, *new.*

It stood on a tripod stand, an odd contrast to the newer machinery itself, and below that was a panel with a switch, quite basic. Something about it seemed too easy. Without allowing another thought to pass through his head, he reached down and flipped.

There is no terror in the explosion, just the anticipation of it. Alfred Hitchcock had said something to that effect, although Edward knew in his thoughts that he was paraphrasing. The only sound that issued was that of the film spinning, and the faint, mechanized hum that it produced. Edward jumped within his own skin. Blue glow, like moonbeams, lasered out of the circular projector.

Edwards eyes followed the light. It seemed to dissipate about halfway through the blackness, odd, considering its strength when standing in proximity. Celluloid blotches appeared on the screen, black and red in color, amorphous and devouring one another, swallowing each other up like hungry blobs.

Grainy images appeared on the screen. It appeared to be of some rural area, shot through grainy sixteen millimeter film. His one semester of film school in Pittsburgh had taught him at least that much. One thing was certain from the first frame, and that was that this was a movie he had never seen before. Barren trees and acreage of landscape. It was beautiful. It was also rather strange.

The film fed itself through the spinning wheel. *Like Rumpelstiltskin weaving hay through his little machine, turning it to gold.* The image projected on the screen began to change—not move—but change, and drastically. The landscapes and trees were still there, but it was the seasons, through the illusion of time lapse photography (or so it seemed) that began to come and go at a great pace. Spring and summer were almost indiscernible, but they were soon replaced by fiery, autumnal colors, and then the desolation and bleakness of bone white winter. Pretty advanced for what appeared to be such an old film. A thought occurred to Edward: he could have been looking at the countryside, but there was something about this that almost seemed prehistoric, a land uncultivated, at the time, by man. *Why am I thinking such ridiculous thoughts? Like cameras existed before civilization.* A voice over snapped him out of his state of confusion.

"In a land before time…"

Edward jumped. The voice was loud, booming. It sounded like the classical voiceover man with the deep voice, the one who was quite prominent in the 90's. It sounded like him, but it *was not* him. He had startled so badly, that the rest of the narrator's sentence became a blur. Land before time? This had to have been some type of prehistoric monster movie, the kind with Claymation dinosaurs designed by Ray Harryhausen and written by Ray Bradbury. Ice age monsters did in fact wonder into the frame; the most realistic Edward had ever seen. *That is not Claymation*, he thought. Saber tooth tigers, American lions, dire wolves, caves bears, wholly rhinos and mastodons—all eerily lifelike, with fur, muscle, flexing, and striations all clearly visible despite the film's fuzzy quality.

How could such an old, low budget film—that had to be what this was—have managed to create such realistic looking extinct animals? These creatures were far beyond the realm of anything that Harryhausen or Bradbury could have imaged, at least on film and not on paper or clay. Even the roaring and trumpeting sounds were too real. The marrow in Edwards spine iced.

Now he kind of wished that he had heard the rest of the narrator's sentence. In a land before time, prehistoric creatures, he quickly figured he had the whole idea. Even still, he could not get over the lifelike quality, and accurate diversity, of the animals.

He watched them stalk and hunt and interact with one another. This went on for what felt like an extended length of time, although he did not realize how long until the sped-up photography kicked in once again. Now, as the animals began to disappear, and were replaced by primitive looking humans wearing clothes and constructing mud huts, the voiceover, like the voice of God, kicked in once more.

"You have read enough books on prehistoric life as a child to know how this works out, Edward," it said.

Edward's stomach dropped. Did that thing just say his name? That was impossible, and absurd.

"What you are seeing is not a film, my son," it continued. "And yes, I *am* talking to you, Edward Johns. What you are seeing is the past—you are looking into the past—of our little town of New Castle, long before the land was corrupted by things like the industrial revolution and this happened…"

The film began to act like it was on speed. A VCR on fast forward, or a DVR tv show on skip. Trees vanished, hills flattened, gullies and ravines became sidewalks and streets.

Edward would have recognized the images anywhere. He was now looking at downtown New Castle, probably during the 20's or 30's, when the steel mills were booming, and the North Hill was the richest district in all of Western Pennsylvania. There were old movies, most of them on YouTube, about this. But these images were taken straight from the history series books, only they were live.

People in old-fashioned garb walked up and down the busy streets. Cars that looked like antique toys trolled on by. The images were not black and white, but full color.

They were beautiful, and he could not look away. For a moment, he almost forgot about the fact that the narrator, or maybe it was the movie itself, seemed to be talking directly to him. The images transitioned from the bustling streets to the steel mills, many of which were now closed, but at the time this was...*shot*...were fully operational, productive, and spewing steam like black clouds out of freight trains.

"Beautiful, is it not?" the voiceover said. "Beautiful, that is, in a corrupted way."

"How are you doing this?" Edward said. "Who are you?"

"I am the father of cinema," the voiceover said. "Specifically, I am *your* father, son."

Edward froze. How had he not recognized the voice of his own dad? That's because it was not his father's voice, at least it hadn't been until that last sentence.

He took his eyes away from the screen, hanging his head in disbelief. Below him, sitting in a seat in the back row of the theater, was a young boy. He looked like he was eating nachos with cheese, Edward's favorite movie theater snack, and he was sipping on an oversized pop, probably coke. The child was watching the screen, seeing the same images that Edward was seeing. He munched and sipped, seemingly fixated on the images. His outfit and reddish-blonde seemed hauntingly familiar, although Edward really couldn't get a great look in the darkness. Who on earth could this child be, and how in the world did he get in here? He poked his head slightly out through the opening, trying to get a better look. He was prepared to call down to him when he heard a voice.

"That's you, just in case you're wondering."

This time, there was no mistaking it. That was his father's voice. It was his father's voice, and it was coming from behind. Edward slowly turned around. Sitting there, in a chair behind the projector was his dad.

"*You're dead,*" Edward whispered. "*You died when I was nine years old. I saw it.*"

A slow smile spread across his father's face. It was the calm, patient grin that he remembered his father making every time he got frustrated. His father had on the same red vest, undershirt, and tie he had been wearing when Edward found him dead in his projectionist booth all those years ago. Brain aneurism. Sometimes symptomatic, but in his father's case, not. Always lethal.

"Death is only temporary," his father said. "Just like anything else. What you think of as 'death' is only relative to life here on earth, which is extremely temporary. The truth of the matter is the state I am in now is eternal. Quite majestic."

"Have you come back to haunt me?" Edward said, unsure.

Again, the slow grin, like a dull burn, spread widely. "You don't remember our relationship very fondly, do you, Edward?"

"I was so young I can barely remember."

"Nine years is a long time to build memories. Maybe you just do not want to remember. After all, if my old man would have brought me into theaters privately to give me first-hand access to movies that other people haven't seen yet, and he died, I would feel pretty bad myself."

Edward felt his throat choking, as if some invisible force were clogging it. "Was it…was it, here?" he said. His father sat with a fixed expression. "It wasn't at this theater? I cannot remember."

His father—his father's *ghost*—paused, as if for dramatic effect. "No, son. It was at Westgate, but I thought it would be more…effective, if you will… if I appeared to you here. Besides, the film I had to show you about the history of our town was better suited for this theater anyway, especially given its own history. You agree?"

"So, what was the point of the film?" Edward said.

"Informational," his father said, crossing his right leg over his left. "Did you not enjoy it? I thought you would."

Edward felt a feeling course through his stomach. It was something he had never felt before. His hands cupped around his waistline. His knees bent. The truth was, he enjoyed, although he simply did not understand.

Again, he asked. "What was the purpose of showing me that film?"

"I'm your *dad*," his father's ghost said. "You should be thrilled to see me again. Instead, you are interrogating me, questioning my motives. What am I the villain here? If you want to bring your family joy, but you must do it from beyond the grave, then does that make you a kind of ghoul?"

"How did you come back?" Edward said.

"Man, you are just full of questions," his father said. "Same old Edward. Inquisitive as always. The truth is, my spirit lingers here—in local cinemas, because that's where I died—so I would have been able to appear in any of them, but since you are here…well, then so am I. being dead, I have access to the past, present, and future all rolled into one, and I can project this access, manifest it, if you will, through cinema."

"So, you wanted to show me the past?" Edward said.

"Not just anybody's past," his father said. "*Our* past. The history of New Castle—the coup of natural megafauna be development (steel mills *and cinemas*)—which you can thus take and put into your book. These images are yours, son."

His father uncrossed his legs and stood up. Edward backtracked an inch or three. His dad looked exactly as he did on the day that Edward found him. *Exactly.* Now, his memory, of that specific incident, was clear as crystal.

His father switched the film off, took the wheel and the camera off the tripod stand and, with the machinery in hand, extended his arms towards Edward. He nodded his head downward, a gesture that suggested *go ahead, grab it, it won't bite you, boy.* Edward felt compelled, but no longer rational or even sane. He slowly reached his arms out towards his father's hands. They were trembling rather badly. Not all ghosts were holy, and ghosts could take any form they pleased, so how did he know that this was not some dark spirit masquerading as his father, taking a form more pleasing? *You're a fool for taking this.*

As he grabbed the camera—the camera that would enable him to print pictures of the prehistoric past, sights that would eventually become New Castle, and Warner Brothers would stand atop mass mammalian graves—he saw his fingertips brush his father's hands. He saw it, but he did not *feel* it. It was like reaching through air, some matter-less, feelingless substance like wind. They slipped right through his father's hands, which now seemed transparent, and grabbed a firm hold of the equipment.

His father seemed pleased. Edward turned around, looking back into the theater. The screen was once again blank, and there was no younger version of himself watching it.

His father grew fainter and fainter, nearly dissipating. Edward wanted to speak, but he had no idea what to say. After his father was no longer visible, his voice sounded from every corner of the small room. *Every time you project that onto a screen, it will be like a looking glass, one that will allow you to travel back in time, safely, and view our sinful corruption of nature. All of this* RICH HISTORY *is cursed by the natural laws, condemned to fail and close forever, but the powers that be have allowed me to give you this tool, so that you may show the present that stands in the place of rightful past.*

Edward was beginning to understand. At least he thought so. He left the room and walked down the stairs, thinking to himself that maybe he could teach Alice and Tim a thing or two historically. Maybe a movie was in order. Who read books anyway?

Contributors

Kristine DeFelice *was born and grew up in New Castle. After spending over 20 years away, she is now a local massage therapist and wellness coach. Kristine enjoys spending time on her stand-up paddle board taking pictures of the wildlife and flowers and trees that can be found in and around the water.*

Betty Hoover DiRisio *was born and raised in Lawrence County, Pennsylvania and graduated from Laurel High School. She attended George Washington University in Washington, DC where she worked on mass tort (asbestos), toxic tort and tobacco litigation for the U.S. Department of the Navy and U.S. Department of Justice. She was also in charge of overseeing environmental compliance for the Navy's six industrial shipyards. Publications include In Hot Pursuit-The Hidden History of the Underground Railroad in Lawrence County, Pennsylvania (2016) and Stage and Screen – The Historic Playhouses of New Castle, Pennsylvania Featuring a History of the Warner Brothers' First Theatre (20160. Betty is currently retired and serves on the Boards of the Lawrence County Historical Society and the Historic Warner Film Center in New Castle while making her home in Fredericksburg, VA.*

MaryAnne Gavrile *is retired from the Crisis Shelter of Lawrence County. She attended Mercyhurst College and graduated from Slippery Rock University with a BS/Ed. She taught alternative education in Zelienople before moving to Las Vegas where she was the marketing director for shows at the Stardust Hotel. Presently, she serves on the Salvation Army Board, the Blueprint Community, and New Castle City Council. She is also a member of Rotary.*

Sam Giannetti *was born in New Castle and raised on Croton Avenue in the 1950s, schooled at St Vitus, Ben Franklin/NeCaHi, Slippery Rock State College and Duquesne University. Sam is a rogue scholar of philosophy, history and life, and earned a living as a workforce development professional and itinerant musician. He is now retired and still living in Lawrence County, PA.*

Denise Yoho Guthery *lived in New Castle until she was 18 and joined the Air Force. That led to a job with the FAA as an Air Traffic Control Specialist and then as a wife and mother. She has lived in California, Texas, and New Mexico. While in New Mexico, she and her husband ran a part-time video business which led to a documentary for the state of New Mexico. When she moved back to PA, she began taking digital photos of the beautiful Amish farms, nature and* *documenting historic landmarks in this area. She has won several awards for her photos in Lawrence and Butler counties. Her photos have been published in The Washington Post, Visit Lawrence County Travel Guides, and other local publications. She originated and coordinates the annual "Details" photo contest for Lawrence County Partners for Preservation. Denise retired a few years ago from Westminster College where she worked in the Admissions Office. She now volunteers at the Historical Society, New Visions, the United Way, and Westminster's Celebrity Series. She carries her camera wherever she goes.*

Kathy Hosler *was born, raised, and still lives in the New Castle area. In 1971, she opened Kathy's Professional Pet Grooming which she operated for 46 years. At present, she is a feature writer for two industry magazines, Groomer To Groomer Magazine and Pet Boarding & Daycare Magazine.*

Joseph Kearney *has been a New Castle attorney for over 42 years with a downtown office. His practice includes family law, estates and wills, and criminal law. He is a resident of Wilmington Township, but was born in Jersey City, New Jersey, and graduated from Syracuse University, both undergraduate and law school. Joseph has two daughters, Lindy and Rachel Kearney. He enjoys reading and being outdoors.*

Dorothy Burchett Knight *was born and raised in western Pennsylvania and is a senior citizen. She moved to New Castle from Knox in 2013 and quickly became adjusted to living here. She is married to Bob Burchett and lives on Sunny Lane. She writes a weekly column for the New Castle News, the Progress News in Emlenton, and the Daily Leader Times in Kittanning. She has had several occupations through the years, from clerical, to restaurant work, to newspaper work and investigative work for a background investigation company. She previously wrote a column for the Clarion News when she lived in Clarion County. She has published a book, titled "Miles and Miracles," available on Amazon. Her hobbies include line dancing, reading, sewing and gardening--especially her flower garden.*

Susan Linville *received a PhD in biology from the University of Dayton and has lectured as adjunct faculty. As a freelance writer, she has published short fiction, newspaper and magazine articles, non-fiction books, blogs, and was a script writer for Indiana University's A Moment of Science Podcast Series. She has published three books on New Castle History including two volumes on historic homes (Historic New Castle Neighborhoods, Vols. 1 and 2) and a reference* book on the Underground Railroad in Lawrence County (*In Hot Pursuit: The Hidden History of the Underground Railroad in Lawrence County, Pennsylvania*, with Elizabeth DiRisio). She manages Pokeberry Press, a micro press, which helps people self-publish books.

Lavonne Lyles was born in New Castle and attended Shenango High School. She worked for Weinshanks Greenhouse and Reliable Luggage. Her interests include History, Gardening, and Poetry.

Jere Moon is currently writing a historical romance set in pre-French and Indian war times about a French fur trader who falls in love with the woman he brings home to raise the son he kidnapped from its Native American mother.

Stephen V. Ramey is a local writer specializing in Flash Fiction (very short stories). He has published more than 200 stories and two collections (*Glass Animals*, Pure Slush Press, and *We Dissolve*, Pokeberry Press). Currently, he's working on a fantasy novel and a novel set in the world of "The Glow" featured in this collection.

Cherisa Rhae is a local artist, librarian, and mother. She lives with her fiancé, John, her toddler son, Asher, and dogs Venus and Akiko. Cherisa uses charcoal and watercolor, as well as chalk pastels. Her subjects often include celestial entities, fairies, mermaids, surrealist landscapes, and smartly dressed animals. Her art has previously been included in *Adultolescence* (2017), and *Dandelion* (2020). Cherisa is excited to add *The Keep* to her publications.

Kat Rodgers is best known as the former owner of the Burg Bar & Grill which she sold to retire. Now she enjoys life. She's presently writing a book, *Visits with Beverly and Others*. She is an active mother of two married daughters, Lisa and Amy. She is a certified teacher with a degree in K-12 and correctional education. Her degrees were earned from Geneva College and Slippery Rock University. She also taught at the Youth Development Center, Ellwood City School District, and retired from Neshannock School District as a learning support teacher after 22 years of teaching.

Randy Ryan is a former power lifter who holds three Pennsylvania state records and a world record in the bench press. He has a Master's in English from Youngstown State University and lives in New Castle with his two dogs, Lilly and Grizzwald. He has published children's (*The Hunter* series) and horror fiction (*Perspectives and Haunted Farms*) and (*Mediums*).

Debra R. Sanchez *has moved over thirty times and has lived in five states and two countries...so far. She and her husband have three adult children, five grandchildren, and a dog and a cat. She leads writing groups and workshops and hosts writing retreats. She is the author of several award-winning books in English and Spanish. Her writing has won awards in various genres, including children's stories, poetry, fantasy, fiction, and creative nonfiction. Several of her other plays and monologues have been produced and published. Other works have been published in literary magazines, newspapers, and anthologies. She is also a translator (English/Spanish) and language tutor/instructor for Spanish and ESL. Visit her webpage:* www.DebraRSanchez.com

Colleen Seegers *is a small-town Western Pennsylvania girl with a love for reading, who dabbled in storytelling and writing from a young age. She worked for most of her career as a registered nurse in California but has now returned home to stay. She has published a book of flash fiction pieces entitled, Snippets.*

David L. Withers *was born at St. Francis Hospital in New Castle, PA in 1955. He grew up on a small farm east of New Castle and graduated from Penn State University in 1978 with a BFA in Graphic Design. David has worked as an art director and creative director for several advertising and catalog companies. He currently lives in Vancouver, Washington.*

Richard G. Yates Jr. *holds a master's degree in Elementary Education and a Bachelor of Science Degree in Psychology. As a Meteorological Observer in the U.S. Army, he learned to appreciate that change is inevitable in both the weather and the human condition. Still, he maintains an unwavering loyalty to the ideals of social justice and the potential for love to win us over. His books include: A Love Book, Greg, Placemat Poems and Vignettes, and Mom.*

Other fine books from
Pokeberry Press

MILES AND MIRACLES

Dorothy Knight Burchett

MEDIUMS

RANDY RYAN

Snippets

Colleen Seegers

A Love Book

Richard G. Yates, Jr.

THE
KEEP

2019

VISIONS OF
NEW CASTLE

EDITORS
SUSAN URBANEK LINVILLE
STEPHEN V. RAMEY

Treasures from the Spirit World

Reverend Karen L Heasley

with

Susan Urbanek Linville

IN HOT PURSUIT

The Hidden History of the
Underground Railroad
in Lawrence County, Pennsylvania

Susan Urbanek Linville, PhD
Elizabeth Hoover DiRisio

Family, Farms & Battlefields:

The Nichols-Newlands and Gray-Heakins Families

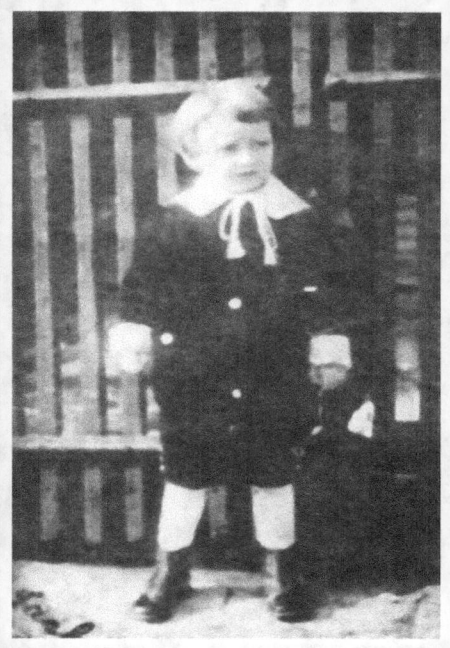

What the Present Generation Owes the Past

John A. Nichols

www.ingramcontent.com/pod-product-compliance
Lightning Source LLC
Chambersburg PA
CBHW070940250626
47159CB00009B/3322